This is a work of fiction. All characters and events are either a product of the author's imagination or used fictitiously, and any resemblance to real people or events is entirely coincidental.

THE WITCH AND THE WYRM

Copyright © 2024 by Beth Alvarez

Cover art by Beth Alvarez

Edited by Amanda Dimer Silva

First Edition: June 2024

ISBN-13: 978-1-952145-31-5

BETH ALVAREZ

*For all the girls
with men like mine,
who, years ago, told me
he wouldn't love me
if I was a coyote.*

One

Ashadow crossed Adelinde's work table. It was enough to obscure her work and her hand froze with a delicate measuring of herbs balanced on a tiny spoon, but a smile graced her lips. The soft breeze through the open window was not enough to carry anything away, and she could afford to wait. "I know you're there, Bastian."

A small laugh answered and a silhouette dimmed her window, blocking most of what light remained. The sun struck his hair and turned it to a warm golden halo around his head, reminiscent of the crown he soon would wear. "You could at least pretend to be surprised." Bastian crossed his arms on the windowsill and leaned forward. He wore a sweet smile, the same one he always greeted her with, but there was an extra sparkle in his eyes.

"What point is there? You told me you were visiting today." She grinned back at him, but tilted her head to one side. "Move over, you're blocking my light."

"Sorry." His smile never faltered as he shuffled to one side of the window and peered in at the mixing bowls and mortar before her. "I brought you a present."

"Did you? Shouldn't I be the one giving you gifts, today?"

Adelinde finished her careful measurements and closed every bottle, jar, and box she'd opened. It was important that she prevent contamination. The careful attention she gave each container definitely had nothing to do with how it allowed her to avoid looking at him.

Bastian was an expert at commanding her attention, though. He held out a sealed envelope between two fingers, careful to keep its shadow from obstructing her work.

It drew her eye, all the same. The king's crest was pressed into the wax.

"I know it's short notice," he said as he wiggled the offering, trying to entice her to take it. "I've already arranged for a dress, so I hope you'll forgive me for telling the tailor to come interrupt you. It'll be everything we ever dreamed of, Adelinde. Tonight, I'll keep my promise."

She sobered. "We were ten, Bas. You don't have to keep promises you made as a child." Nor could he, anymore. The thought roused the grief she had tried to bury and she struggled to tamp it down.

"A promise is a promise, no matter when it's made. And I dare say I'm more in love with you now than I was the day you saved my life." He leaned forward to catch her eye.

She refused to give him the satisfaction. She could never help but smile when she locked eyes with him, his good nature too infectious to resist. So she kept her head down and pressed the pestle into her mortar full of herbs. The gold rings on her fingers clicked against the stone. "You were also delirious."

"And you're even more angelic now than when I saw you in that fever haze," he teased, though his voice grew more subdued. He felt it too, then. The unlikeliness that things would go as planned.

There had been a time she believed they might have the sort of happily-ever-after ending he'd promised. He'd been a second son, little more than an extra layer of protection for his father's rule, unnecessary and unimportant.

Then his brother had fallen to the dragon, and everything had changed.

She still hadn't taken the envelope from his fingers, so he reached in to leave it on her work table. She already knew what was inside; an invitation to the ball that night, celebrating his birthday, his ascent to heir, and his impending engagement, all at once.

And a king-to-be could never marry a mere herbalist.

"I can't come, Bastian. I can't watch you celebrate your engagement to someone else." It hurt her heart even to think of it.

His smile faded until his mouth held a sour twist. "I am not proposing to Florina. I don't care what agreement my father has with her mother. She couldn't prevent the beast from taking my brother, why should I believe she has the power to stop it now?"

Adelinde didn't know how to argue, nor did she want to. Neither one of them had the power to undo the king's decisions, and she had already cried enough tears over the loss of what she'd foolishly let herself desire.

Her silence wounded him, for when he spoke again, his tone was plaintive. "Please come, Adelinde. If it's the only gift you give me, it will be enough." He pressed a fingertip to the edge of the envelope and slid it closer to the stone mortar she gripped with both hands.

"I have a gift for you already," she replied. It was what lay in the bowl before her, waiting to be mixed. He knew nothing of her work, aside from that it had saved him once, and would not recognize the ingredients or their purpose. Her throat tightened and she swallowed against it to find the will to speak. "I'll come tonight, so I can give it to you."

He brightened, and the sparkle it restored to his blue eyes made her chest ache. "Thank you. It's all I really want. *You're* all I want."

In spite of all her sensibilities, the declaration made her heart flutter.

"I'll be there," she promised, though it was the last thing she wanted to do.

"Thank you," he repeated. "And I love you, Adelinde. My Nightingale. Nothing will ever change that."

The smile she responded with was tight-lipped, but he'd already decided he'd won.

Bastian pushed himself back until only his hands remained on the windowsill. "Won't you say it back?"

"You're blocking my light," she replied.

He shifted until he obstructed as much of it as he could. "I know you're thinking it."

Any other time, she would have responded to his teasing with a playful swat and sent him on his way. This time, all she did was sigh and lift her head to look him in the eye. "I love you, too, Bastian." She had since girlhood. He'd fallen in love with her the day she'd helped her mother save him, but she'd fallen not long after, when he'd returned to offer her a wildflower bouquet.

Bastian accepted her answer with a grin and let go of the windowsill. "I'll see you tonight."

"Of course." She tried to put on a cheerful face as she watched him retreat through her garden, but she couldn't hold it for long, nor could she let herself stare as he departed. It was the last time they would be meeting like that, with him appearing at her window with some small gift in his hand. No matter what he'd promised, his father had all but publicly declared Bastian's newly arranged engagement. He'd always been a prince, but now he would be the crowned heir of Ceresia.

She might as well have been a worm.

Adelinde blinked hard as she pounded the herbs in her mortar to a fine dust. She'd had weeks to accept her childish dream had been shattered, and she refused to let another tear fall. Instead, she trained her attention on the mortar and pestle and the steady rhythm they made as she worked, the cadence accentuated by the merry clinking of the splint rings on her fingers.

She had just pressed the cork into the finished potion's bottle when the tailor arrived.

The woman frowned and gave her a once-over as she dragged a heavy trunk through the doorway. "He didn't know any of your measurements," she announced instead of offering a greeting or an introduction. "So let me begin by saying I'm a seamstress, not a miracle worker."

"I'll be happy to be in anything suitable for a ballroom, given how little time he's afforded you." Adelinde dried her hands and put away her work towel before she helped the tailor lift the trunk onto the low couch in the cottage's main room. There was still plenty of sunlight, but proper alterations took ages, and the event began at sundown.

The tailor sniffed in approval. "Well, as long as you can be realistic. Here, these are the options I've brought." One by one, she drew dresses from the trunk, each of them a rich, autumnal shade that would flatter Adelinde's dark hair and pale complexion. All of them were fine silk, and any would be appropriate.

Adelinde chose one without much thought. It didn't matter what she wore; it would all end the same, with her excusing herself from the festivities the moment her sweetheart's engagement was announced. "This will be fine. Or whichever one is the easiest for you to alter for fit."

"Very well. Put it on and we'll begin." The tailor put the other dresses aside and took a box of thread from her trunk while Adelinde ducked behind the dressing screen that hid her bed from the rest of the main room.

The gown she'd chosen almost fit and wouldn't take much adjustment. Adelinde brushed her hands down her front and for a fleeting moment, she allowed herself to dream that it was her engagement party, instead. Then she sighed and stepped out from behind the screen.

"I think it's close," she said as she squeezed the sides of the bodice to pull it tight across her body.

"Good, because we haven't much time to make it perfect." The tailor strode around her, pinching fabric and inserting pins until it fit like a second skin.

Adelinde let her gaze drift back to the finished potion on her work table and almost told her not to worry. Any dress would be fine. It wasn't as if Bastian would remember her, after tonight.

The palace perched on a hilltop overlooking the valley, taller than any of the trees that surrounded Adelinde's cottage at the edge of the woods. She'd made the trek to the palace walls several times since Bastian had come into her life, but she'd never been welcomed beyond a simple parlor where messengers were received. Well, she conceded, that wasn't true; she and her mother had been invited to appear before the king after they'd saved Bastian. King Bernhard had thanked them as they knelt as his feet, but it had been nothing more than formality, and he had never spoken to them again.

Would he remember who she was? Adelinde tried to imagine herself bowing before the king in the ballroom. She couldn't fathom what such a space might look like, though she tried to imagine it as the carriage wound its way up the meandering trails.

The carriage had arrived to collect her shortly after the tailor finished alterations. Adelinde was grateful; she hadn't stopped to consider how she was supposed to arrive at the palace in a presentable state if she had to walk the whole way. Bastian had always been thoughtful, though. This was just one more reason to love him—and one more reason to mourn.

The tall, pale spires of the palace cast cold shadows across the dozens of carriages that circled through the courtyard, depositing guests by the door. Adelinde shifted to the edge of her seat as her carriage took its place in the line of arrival, the potion she'd brewed as a gift for the prince cradled in both her hands.

Her stomach lurched as the carriage stopped before the palace entryway. The driver descended and the carriage rocked as he moved, which didn't help.

"Here we are, Miss," the driver announced as he opened the door and offered a hand to help her out.

She held the rounded glass bottle to her stomach with one hand and accepted the help with the other. "Thank you, but where do I go from here?" The hallways inside would be harder to navigate than the woods where she'd grown up, the stone walls unfamiliar and imposing.

"I suppose you just follow everyone else." The driver winked, which made her blush, but it was fair for him to tease her. It was a stupid question, given how many people filtered in through the palace's front doors.

"Thank you," she replied, unsure what else to say, and when she hurried up the stairs to follow another guest through the doors, no one seemed to notice.

Others drifted in behind her, all of them carrying gifts of some sort. All of them seemed to know where they were going. Adelinde kept pace with them, but when the hallway opened into the grand ballroom, she slowed to a halt and allowed herself to gape.

She'd expected something cold and austere, given the looming height and smooth white walls of the castle's exterior. Instead, the grand hall before her was nothing shy of lavish. Bold patterns in bright colors decorated the walls between ornate murals that sprawled across the plaster beneath balconies with gold-trimmed balustrades. Half a dozen chandeliers as large as the entire main room of her cottage glowed overhead, wrought with gilt and filled with pale white candles. Plush benches lined both long walls of the hall and noblewomen in glorious gowns lounged beneath tall, arched windows.

"Adelinde!" Bastian's excited voice carried over the murmur of partygoers and their conversations. He squeezed between two clusters of people and jogged over to join her. His smile was dazzling. The crown on his head made her heart ache.

"Did I miss it? Am I late?" Her eyes stayed fixed on that crown, even as he reached for her hands. She avoided his touch, still clutching the bottle.

"No, no. My father just—ah, he's made this whole thing a mess. Heldin demanded I be crowned and recognized before all this, and you know how my father is when she's involved." His lip curled with distaste and he waved a hand, as if the woman's name had left a foul scent in the air.

Adelinde didn't blame him. She would have preferred not to hear the witch's name at all. Sorceress, she corrected herself in her thoughts; Heldin called herself a sorceress, and anyone who suggested otherwise received a harsh lecture at the very least. "Of course she did," Adelinde said. "She wants the heir to propose to her daughter, not a second prince."

"No one cares what she wants," Bastian grumbled.

"Your father does." Her hands tightened on the potion bottle until her knuckles grew pale.

It was only then that he noticed it. "What's that? Where are your rings?"

Her throat tightened, but she made herself smile. She hadn't wanted to leave the delicate golden splints behind, but it hadn't seemed right to wear jewelry that had been a gift from the prince, tonight of all nights. "A gift." She held out the bottle and gave it a tilt, its thin, reddish contents swishing against the sides. "For you. To make today easier."

A gentle furrow drew itself between his brows. "What do you mean?"

Adelinde pressed it into his hands. "You know I love you,

Bastian. Your father has already made his intentions clear. The fact you're already wearing that crown proves it. I just want to make it easier for you. So when you see her..." She motioned to the potion as she let it go and stepped back, her fingers laced together against her stomach. "Drink it. It'll help."

He looked down at the bottle in his grasp and when he realized what it was, his confusion twisted into dismay. "A love potion? I don't want to love her, Adelinde! I don't want anything to do with her."

"Don't make it harder on yourself than it has to be." She retreated another step and held out her hands to stop him when he tried to follow her.

"Take it back." Bastian held the bottle at arm's length and tried to push it into her hands.

She shook her head. "I'm just trying to help. You have to. You know you have to."

An unfamiliar light of anger flared in his eyes and he shoved the potion bottle against her chest and let go. She barely caught it.

"I will not," he replied, each word clearly enunciated. He shook his head as he paced backwards, then turned to storm across the ballroom.

Her heart lurched. "Bastian, wait." She trailed after him, clutching the potion until her fingers ached. She hadn't expected him to be happy about it, but she'd pictured this going differently. A moment of sad acceptance, an example of his usual social grace as he took her offering and resigned himself to the fate his father had chosen. Neither one of them wanted this, but what hope was there to escape? Their country was under attack. The sorceress Heldin was their last hope, and she had already named her price. The remaining prince's hand for her daughter. Then, she would destroy the dragon that threatened their lives. The same dragon had taken Bastian's brother, and Adelinde cursed the beast and every last scale on its miserable hide.

"Wait," Adelinde begged. She reached for his sleeve, but he

snatched his arm out of her grasp and darted through the crowds. People had begun to turn and look at them, their eyes weighted with judgment and a hunger that made her skin crawl. Every moment she now spent in the palace was fuel for gossip, for wicked, tormenting words about the poor, foolish herbalist's daughter who thought she could have a prince.

She lost track of Bastian among the partygoers and stopped in her tracks to strain on tip-toe and hope some sight of him might resurface. She turned in place, her stomach tying itself in knots as whispers spread between the nobles around her.

A moment later, he reappeared beside his father at the edge of the musicians' arcade. Confusion, then surprise crossed King Bernhard's face, and the two of them vanished through a nearby doorway.

Adelinde gripped the potion bottle and fought back a grimace.

She'd thought he understood. She didn't want him to marry Heldin's daughter any more than he wanted to. For years, she'd believed his promises they would be wed, that his father wouldn't mind because Erich was the one who would take the throne.

Now Erich was dead, and as long as the dragon that killed him survived, Bastian—and all of Ceresia—was at risk.

Abruptly, the musicians stopped. Adelinde spun back toward their stage and froze when the king climbed onto it and raised a hand, calling for attention.

"Well," King Bernhard began, and the crowds grew quiet. "It seems my son is eager to begin the night with the real celebration."

The knots in her stomach twisted tighter. "Don't," she whispered, knowing Bastian wouldn't hear her or even see the pleading in her eyes as she watched him kneel on the steps before his father's feet.

"Tonight, on his twentieth birthday, Prince Bastian has been crowned as heir. With him lies the hope and future of Ceresia.

And tonight, his legacy begins. His bride has been chosen, and with this new alliance, hope abounds. Much have we struggled this year. Much has been lost. But justice will arise, for the dragon's death is nigh."

Cheers and applause rose from the crowd. Adelinde's nose crinkled. It wasn't even a good speech.

King Bernhard motioned for them to settle as he produced something from beneath his fur-trimmed cape. Murmurs of wonder and appreciation swept through the people.

Adelinde's throat tightened until she could scarcely breathe.

The crystal lily in the king's hand was a remarkable treasure, a symbol of the kingdom passed down through generations. A proposal gift that should have been given to Erich's chosen bride, the future queen. The king lowered it to Bastian's hands, and the prince rose. Somewhere to the side, people shuffled about and pushed a familiar young woman to the front. Florina, the sorceress's daughter, smoothed her skirts and stood perfectly straight.

Bastian curled his hand around the glittering flower's stem. "The dragon's destruction is nigh," he said, his voice carrying across the silent ballroom as he stood. "I am honored by the crown you have given me, Father, and I will strive to deserve it. But I have chosen my own bride."

The king's mouth twitched and his brows drew together.

"Don't," Adelinde breathed. She tried to retreat, but she couldn't move, as if her feet were frozen in place. Her knees trembled, weak as water.

Bastian turned and all around them, eyes widened and faces fell as he strode toward the crowd with the crystal lily cradled in his hand. Guests stepped aside, clearing a path as he moved. "I've made a promise, one I mean to fulfill. If a king cannot be trusted to keep his word, then how can the people trust when I say the dragon will die? The monster will be destroyed, but when its death comes and the loss of my brother is finally avenged, it will be my hand that strikes down the beast. And when I marry…" He stopped before Adelinde and people moved back, leaving the two of them in a space of their own. "It will be to the woman I truly love, because I cannot live a lie."

Tears stung her eyes as he sank to one knee and offered the crystal lily before her.

"Adelinde," he murmured, his voice rough and his face pinched with concern. "My precious Nightingale. Let me keep my promise. Please."

She didn't get a chance to respond.

"How dare you?" A high, shrill voice broke the silence, its words filled with rage.

The swarms of people parted as partygoers shrank away from the speaker.

Adelinde's heart sank at sight of the woman, not old enough in appearance to command her station, too regal to be anyone else.

If only witches were like those in the stories, nothing but bitter, ugly old women instead of the striking and powerful figure she beheld now. She flinched back, expecting the witch to sweep toward them and strike her down.

King Bernhard made a smoothing motion with both hands, but the witch raised a finger before he could speak.

"You," Heldin snarled as she paced forward, her step slow and measured. "You were sworn to me. To our alliance. How dare you? Does your brother's death mean nothing to you?"

Whispers swept the audience and Adelinde cursed herself. She should have made him wait that afternoon, should have given him the potion then and refused to attend the ball. She gripped the potion bottle until her knuckles turned white.

"His death means everything." Bastian raised his voice, ensuring everyone heard him. "My brother died for nothing, with nothing, and has left nothing behind but us. My brother's death made me certain that no life was worth living without joy."

The witch scoffed. "And a dragon laying waste to your kingdom brings you joy? Seeing your people suffer brings joy?"

He shook his head. "No. But Adelinde is the only thing that does."

Adelinde squeezed her eyes shut and willed herself not to cry. He'd told her as much a thousand times or more, but to hear it spoken that way, before all the nobles of his father's court, was different. It should have been anything but heartrending, but there was no stopping the way she shattered now.

Heldin's face twisted with anger. "You will know your place, child. You bow your head. You do as I command. And when you seek my forgiveness, you will crawl on your belly to have it!" She raised a hand, finger skyward, and screams burst around them as magic lanced the air, harsh and acrid.

"No!" Adelinde leaped forward, but it was too late. The thousand flames on the chandeliers overhead winked out as Bastian curled in on himself with a gasp, and darkness swallowed the ballroom.

Shrieks of terror rose, even as the king barked orders and the ballroom burst into panic. Adelinde landed on her knees and one empty hand and yelped at the impact. "Bastian!" she gasped as she dropped the potion bottle and groped for him in the dark, her hands finding nothing but skirts and legs of people as they tried to flee.

Cold wind gusted through from the balcony doors and the chandeliers flared back to life. She blinked against the sudden light.

"Enough!" The king roared.

Feet stilled, and something brushed the side of Adelinde's thumb. Magic crackled against her skin at its touch, enough to make her stomach lurch.

The witch Heldin was gone, and where her sweet childhood love had been, there was nothing but an earthworm on the floor.

Three

Adelinde crawled forward, shielding the pitiful creature on the palace floor as tears brimmed against her eyelashes. This was her fault. Her doing. Her eyes darted every which direction until she spotted the potion bottle, just out of arm's reach. She lunged after it and pried the cork from its top. Her fingers bent uncomfortably and she bit down on her tongue.

She should have given it to him sooner, she told herself again. Forget that afternoon; she should have given it to him weeks ago, when Heldin first proposed the marriage between her daughter and the soon-to-be crown prince.

Adelinde upended the bottle and dumped its contents on the floor, then reached for the worm. He twisted and flailed when she touched him. Magic still stung her fingertips, but it was less than that first brush had been.

"Bastian," she whispered as she scooped him into her palm.

There was no mistaking it, not with the magic that burned in his fragile body, and she thought she would be ill.

"Where is he?" King Bernhard's bellow echoed against the arched ceiling.

She crammed the earthworm into the bottle and pushed the

cork back into place with the heel of her palm, then tried to sink into the crowd. Others made for the doors and she lost herself between them as the king's voice rose to split the room.

"Bastian!" Bernhard roared.

Adelinde gripped the bottle tighter and ran the moment she reached the hallway.

When you seek my forgiveness, you'll crawl on your belly to have it.

Heldin's words echoed in Adelinde's head and she barked a harsh, humorless laugh.

A worm.

The witch had turned him into a *worm*.

Blind, spineless, voiceless—everything they wanted him to be, fearful and browbeaten by the threat of the witch's power.

And yet he was useless to them like this. Rumors of the witch's fast temper were common, but to spite herself by cursing the prince? Adelinde could hardly believe it.

"Which means she has to fix this," she whispered to herself as she hurried through the palace alongside all the other departing guests. She was not the only one who ran, but her step carried purpose.

She *had* to fix it. It was her responsibility; it had been her folly that had landed them here, her inability to let go.

Yet Bastian was not innocent, either. He knew his place, knew what was expected of him and what task he'd been given. He had shirked his duty, too—yet as her hands cradled the skin-warmed glass of the potion bottle close against her stomach, she could not blame him for what he'd done.

He loved her.

He'd defied his father for her.

Saving him from that mistake was the least she could do.

Adelinde stopped for breath the moment she reached the courtyard. Carriages and saddled horses crowded the space. Footmen and drivers argued over who deserved to go next. Amid the fuss and furor, it was easy to slip away, and she crept between the carriages and coaches as she collected her thoughts. Her soft silk slippers whispered against the stone, thin enough to let her feel every rough pebble underfoot. The discomfort was grounding, and she focused on it until her mind was clear and her feet carried her beyond the palace gates.

There was only one solution, she decided as she stopped at the side of the road and gazed out across the darkened woods. She would find the witch, apologize for her part in the mistake, provide a new love potion and step aside.

Of course, finding the witch was the first trial. Heldin lived in the forest; the village folk went out of their way to avoid the woods north of the palace. How far north, though, she didn't know. Nor was she certain the witch would be there at all. For all Adelinde knew, the woman already resided in the palace. Then again, that made little sense; if she already had access to the palace, she'd know how to sink her claws into the king. So far, she'd only managed to snare Bastian in her schemes.

"For a daughter we know nothing about," she murmured to herself.

Where had Florina been, the moment the curse was laid? Adelinde had never so much as looked. Now, the unknown needled at her in a way that made her feel petty.

Had Florina sneered, the way Heldin did? Had she looked upon her betrothed with smugness when he was punished for slighting her? It was easier to imagine she had. Bastian had not mentioned the young woman often, and Adelinde liked to believe it was because he did not care to know her, never mind marry her.

"But that sort of petty thinking won't get you out of this mess, will it?" She muttered to herself as she trudged off the road and into the woods. The forest at night was hardly a proper place for a lady in a ball gown, but she couldn't imagine things could get any worse. What was there to fear when her goal was to run afoul of the most powerful witch those woods had ever known?

She hadn't gone far before the lights of the palace faded away behind her, and the shadows of the forest grew deeper. "So we'll need a light," she concluded.

Adelinde considered that for a time, then scanned the ground. Surely there would be a stone out here that was capable of producing sparks, and for all that her slippers were dainty, they had those garish buckles on the strap across the toes. One of those would be sufficient for striking sparks, no doubt.

She turned in circles until she found a rock with a texture she thought might work. A sturdy branch to be the base of her torch came next. A strip off the white underskirt would work for fuel, but that needed both hands to tear free. She put down her rock and branch, then sat the round glass bottle beside them.

The cloth was tougher than she expected. Adelinde gritted her teeth and strained, but no matter how she pulled or twisted, the fabric would not tear. She'd need something to cut it, then. A sharper rock might get it started. She leaned forward until she could crawl, her knees grinding dark stains into the front of her silk gown as she ran her hands across the earth in search of something to use.

Leaves rustled behind her and she froze.

There wouldn't be people out here this time of night—no one but the witch, and Adelinde doubted the woman had vanished in the blink of an eye only to trudge through the darkened forest alone. Never mind that it had been so soft. An animal in the leaves, nothing large enough to harm her.

The soft *tink* of something tapping glass tore a gasp from her throat and Adelinde spun back. A black shadow shuffled around the potion bottle, then tapped with its beak again.

A crow.

"Leave him alone!" She lunged forward and seized her branch, then swung at the bird.

It leaped back with a croak, its black wings spread.

Adelinde swung at it again.

"Hey, hey!" The crow chided.

She shrieked and fell on her backside.

"Oh, we're doing this, then, are we? Go on ahead, keep screaming. See if that helps you at all." The bird scoffed and shook his head.

"You speak!" she cried.

"Ah, yes, thank you for noticing. I was beginning to think no one would." His voice was strong, clear, and his sarcasm bit.

Adelinde stared, wide-eyed. "Are you one of them, then? One of the fae?"

The bird made a noise that was halfway between a laugh and a caw. "If I was one of the fae, do you think I'd show up like this? As a crow, instead of some stunningly handsome fae king to sweep a girl like you off your feet and whisk you off to my realm?" His feathers ruffled and he shook his head. "Pah. No, I'm just an unlucky fool like the one you've got in that bottle." His beak flicked toward it.

That should have been the last thing to soothe her nerves, but Adelinde found herself relaxing. "You're a man?"

"Not anymore. But it seems like I got off better than this fellow, didn't I?" The crow hopped toward the bottle again.

Slowly, Adelinde reached for the bottle. She curled her fingers around its neck and pulled it close. "How did you know he's a person?"

"The magic stings when it's fresh. Scents the air, like the heat after a lightning strike. You ever smelled that? Ah, maybe not. You don't want to, anyway. It doesn't smell good, and being hit with magic doesn't feel much better than a lightning bolt." His feathers ruffled and something that resembled a shudder coursed through him.

She stared at the bird as a crease drew itself between her brows. "Did the magic bring you?" The likelihood of encountering another cursed man the moment she set foot in the woods was so improbable, it made the hair on the back of her neck prickle.

"Ah..." He brushed a wing to one side, a remarkably human

gesture of dismissal. "Sort of. I've been following the sorceress for a while. Keeping enough distance she doesn't see me, but I wasn't far off when I felt her do... whatever it is she's done to your bloke, there. Who is he, anyway?"

"Who are you?" she retorted.

"Fair question. You can call me Aldram, and I've... been stuck this way a few years." He turned his head, as if to avert his eyes. The gesture struck her as sheepish.

"I'm Adelinde." It was not what he'd asked, but what difference did it make? "I'm an herbalist."

Aldram gave a thoughtful hum. "Potions won't help you with this, I'm afraid. Or maybe they will, but it would have to be something Heldin makes. I've been after her for years, since... well. Let's just say curse breaking isn't easy."

She hadn't assumed it would be. "That's why I'm hoping I can convince her to undo this." It wasn't as if Bastian would be useful to the witch as a worm, anyway. "I'm assuming she'll have gone home after what happened at the ball, but I'm afraid I don't know where 'home' is."

"Ah! Well, convenient for you, then. I happen to know exactly where the sorceress lives." Aldram thrust himself from the ground with a good flap of his wings and climbed to perch on a low branch. "I'd be happy to show you."

Adelinde climbed to her feet. "For what price?"

"Price? What makes you think there's a price?" the bird asked, and if she hadn't been sure before, the breezy way he asked made her certain.

"Because I'm not totally convinced you aren't one of the fae."

Aldram let out a cackle. "You're less foolish than your sweetheart, then. Yes, I'll take you. But in exchange, I want to hear everything that's said, and if she sends you off on some task to break his curse, I want help breaking mine, too."

"That's a bold request for a bird who's only offering directions." She lifted her chin and gave him a challenging stare.

"All right, all right. How about this, then? I take you to see the old witch, and if she gives you a quest or whatever it is witches do, I'll help you get through it. In exchange, you'll help with mine. Deal?" He fluttered to a new branch, a few paces away.

She followed. "Don't you have your own sweetheart to help you out of your bind?"

"Ah..." Aldram tilted his head skyward, then shuffled his wings. "That's a bit of a story on its own. The short version is, no. I've got nobody left. Which is why I've been out here, following the sorceress around in hopes of seeing something useful. And you're very useful, dove, aren't you?" He turned one too-knowing eye her direction.

Adelinde swallowed. "Very well, then. Let's go."

"Wonderful. You won't regret this, girly, I'm the best friend you could make." The crow fluttered ahead to the next tree. "You're lucky I'm just a man and not fae, though."

"Why is that?" She picked up her skirts in one hand and followed him through the dark, careful to keep the potion bottle —and Bastian—close to her heart.

He cackled. "You already gave me your name."

<h1 style="text-align:center">Four</h1>

Several miles north of the hill where the palace huddled, now dark and foreboding, the forest grew thick. Aldram dropped from the treetops to flap from bush to bush instead of flying between the trees.

"We're getting close, now," the crow said, his voice low. "Best watch your footing."

"Why?" Adelinde asked. "Should I be worried about traps?"

The crow gave a chuckle. "I wouldn't put it past her. That witch has been known to do worse. Just look at me."

She supposed that was a fair point. There was Bastian to think about, too—the poor worm in the bottle that she still cradled in both hands. It was easier to hold him like that with the crow leading the way. All she had to do was worry about walking. Her fingertips trailed over the smooth glass, her touch both tentative and thoughtful. "Do you really think she'll let him go? As long as I do something in return?" She didn't know what went into curse breaking, but the hope an apology might be enough had already evaporated.

"That's impossible for me to say." Aldram gave his wings a little flutter. It was something of a nervous tic, she decided, something he kept doing whenever he didn't know how to respond or which direction to go.

She couldn't help but wonder if he was always so jittery. Or at least, if he had been when he was a human. "She has to help him though, right? She needs him. She has to help him for that reason alone."

The crow stopped and gave her a curious, if doubtful look. "Why would a sorceress need a hopeless little worm like your sweetheart? If he's foolish enough to make her angry, then I can't imagine how she would need him."

"It was part of their deal."

"Witches don't need the people they make deals with," Aldram grumbled. "I thought she needed me too, and look where I am now."

"But it wasn't just for her," Adelinde said. "That has to mean something, right? It was her daughter. He was supposed to marry Florina. He was never supposed to propose to me."

The crow gave himself an ugly little jolt. "Now, hold up. Marriage proposals? To the sorceress's daughter? To be that important, he'd have to be—"

"Prince Bastian," she said before he could finish.

Aldram almost sputtered. "Prince Bastian? Prince Bastian! Oh, Divine mercy, you've done it now!"

Her cheeks heated, though if it was from embarrassment or anger, she didn't know. "It wasn't my doing! I told him to marry her, like he was supposed to."

"And he proposed to you instead? The little herbalist? Right in front of Heldin's face? Oh, no wonder that curse magic bit so hard when I tasted it on the air." His feathers ruffled and he shook as if to rid himself of water.

Adelinde hardly cared. Whether the magic used had been great or small didn't matter. It had transformed the one she loved, either way. "She was angry. I think she overreacted. But she still needs him, because he's the only possible heir left. She has to be willing to cooperate if it means getting back that opportunity."

"You'd better thank your stars she left you alive so you can ask," the crow said. "And weep for your beloved, because he hasn't been so lucky. Heldin has the power to smite you. To smite any one of us. If she's left him alive, it's because he still has a chance to be useful."

To crawl on his belly and beg forgiveness, the witch had said. Adelinde stroked the glass bottle. "Is that why you're still alive?" she asked softly.

Aldram craned his neck to look back at her. "Best we move along, girly. Watch your feet."

The crow shared no more chatter and asked no more questions as they worked their way through the dense part of the forest. Eventually, the trees gave way to a slow-moving stream, and from there, a narrow path climbed back into the woods.

"This way." Aldram landed on the path and hopped about until he faced her.

Adelinde slipped off her shoes and carried them in one hand so she could cross the stream. Gravel coated the bottom, but mud still squelched between her toes, and she didn't have enough hands to keep her skirts from getting wet. Her gown was ruined beyond recognition now. A fine way for Bastian's last gift to end.

As soon as she reached the other bank, the bird flitted up to her shoulder. He was heavier than she'd expected and she gasped at the prick of his claws.

"Sorry," he muttered, his voice low beside her ear. "Now, listen. You just take yourself right up this path and take care of business. Strike your deal, or whatever else you need, and if you survive, you come right back down to this stream and I'll be waiting for you here."

"You're not coming with me?"

"I can't take you any farther, no. Heldin's likely to blast me out of the sky if she sees me winging about." He flicked a wing and the brush of his feathers against her skin tickled unpleasantly.

Adelinde cast a doubtful look up the path. "How much farther is it?"

"Close enough you'd best keep your voice down." His dropped to a whisper, as if to make a point. "Good luck, girly. I'll be waiting for you." He thrust off her shoulder and winged his way into the trees before she could protest.

She squared her shoulders and sucked in a deep breath. "Well, we've come this far. We've got to see it through." She didn't know whether she spoke to herself or to Bastian. Could he even hear her? She didn't know. Worms were blind, but she was unsure whether or not they were deaf. She preferred to think that he could still hear everything she said.

The path was hard-packed beneath her bare feet, and she did not hurry to put on her shoes. Her toes were still muddy and her dress wet, and if there weren't any twigs or leaves in her hair by now, she'd be stunned.

All the more pitiful she felt, then, when the forest gave way to a clearing and the witch's home came into view.

It had always been easy to assume the woman lived in some eerie hovel, or a moss-covered cottage surrounded by thorny plants. Instead, the castle-like manor that rose before her was as stately as Heldin herself, its windows aglow with candles that illuminated the manicured gardens around them.

Adelinde lingered on the path until a shadow passed through a room on the other side of one of those windows. Her feet itched to run, but she made herself stride to the stone steps in front of the door, where she paused to slip into her shoes. They were gritty and odd with the mud between her toes, but it was better than being barefoot.

The door bore a large iron ring, so she seized it and gave a single hard knock. The sound echoed, heavy and hollow, and she waited for the witch to answer.

Instead, the hinges groaned as the door swung open of its own accord.

"Enter," something rasped, not quite a voice, yet unmistakably a word.

Adelinde swallowed hard and stepped inside.

The door swung shut and latched behind her. She glanced back, but given what she knew of the grand house and its inhabitant, it was little surprise. She braced herself and drew a breath. "I'm here to see the—the owner of this estate," she corrected herself halfway through. Whether or not it was true, calling the woman a witch to her face was profoundly unwise.

Directly in front of her, another door opened. "Come in, then," the same strange, rasping voice replied.

The room beyond was dark and quiet. Adelinde's whisper-soft footsteps and the rustle of her dirt-stained silk dress struck her as loud as she crept through what appeared to be a parlor, though the stale air promised there had been no guests in a long time. To the left, another door creaked open and let light pour through.

"Come along, then," a woman sighed. "I haven't got all night."

"Thank you, my lady," Adelinde said as she crept into the small study. Bookshelves lined the space, every one of them crammed full. Books and scrolls and papers sat piled on the floor, crowding a narrow ring of a path that encircled the similarly overflowing desk where the woman sat.

Heldin had been more frightening in the ballroom, when anger and power contorted her face. Now she merely looked tired. Heavy lines skirted her eyes and mouth and strands of her graying hair had come out of place to stand like corkscrews atop her head. The witch regarded her with a stern frown before her brow furrowed. "Who are you?" Slowly, her gaze slid down to the potion bottle. "What have you brought?"

A nervous flutter rolled over in Adelinde's chest. The woman didn't recognize her? It had scarcely been a few hours. Instead of answering the first question, she simply held out the glass bottle with its front exposed, revealing the worm that twisted languidly inside. "This is... Prince Bastian."

The witch's eyebrows rose.

Adelinde's mouth had gone dry. She swallowed hard, though it brought no relief, and tried to look sensible as she explained. "I've come to apologize for what he did at the ball. I know what he was supposed to do. I didn't want him to dishonor his responsibilities."

"And so you brought him to me?" Heldin sounded amused, or maybe curious, and she lowered the paper in her hands to her desk.

"To apologize," Adelinde repeated. "And to ask your help in changing him back. Whatever I must do to help him, simply let me know and I will do it."

The witch snickered. "You think having him will be that easy, do you?"

"No, my lady. I would change him back so he may wed your daughter, as promised." The words threatened to choke her, but Adelinde kept her face serene as she spoke.

Heldin's amusement only grew. "The poor boy. You must care for him so little, to come to me and give him away the very night he proclaimed his love for you."

Adelinde smiled back at her, though grimly. "On the contrary, it's my love for him that brings me here. I would far rather see him healthy, well, and wed to another than to keep him in a bottle and have him all for myself."

For a time, the witch merely stared at her. Then, at last, she sighed and leaned back in her chair. "Perhaps it was harsh. As much as I would like to teach him a lesson, he is still necessary, isn't he?" The melodious tones of her voice sent a chill down Adelinde's spine, but the pensive way the woman looked at the bottle—and the pitiful worm trapped inside it—was sincere. "I should have chosen something milder. That sort of transformation will require reagents to undo."

"Then I'll retrieve them for you," Adelinde said. "Whatever you need."

"Yes," Heldin said with a cold smile. "You certainly will."

That the witch would agree so easily left her unsettled, but what other choices were there? Adelinde offered a single nod. "What must I bring?"

"Three things, and your help for each step. First, I will need you to bring a particular flower with curative properties. You will help me prepare it, once everything has been collected."

"You mean like preparation of a potion?" Adelinde's garden hosted many flowers, but she dared not hope it would be as easy as going home to pick something.

"Precisely. Are you familiar with such practices?" Heldin regarded her with curiosity and for the first time, it felt as if the woman had truly noticed her.

Adelinde nodded. "It's my job. I make curatives for the village."

"Then you should know a great deal about flowers," the witch said. "You are familiar with the wyrmstooth lily?"

The crystal blossom Bastian had presented as part of his proposal sprang to mind and Adelinde's heart sank. "Wyrmstooth lilies are extinct."

Heldin waved a hand as if to bat away the claim. "Certainly not, they are merely exceptionally rare. The last known garden where they grew was at a church, far to the north, near the border Ceresia shares with Athanor. You will need to go there and retrieve at least one full blossom, although three would be better. How are your foraging skills? To feed yourself along the way?"

Adelinde hesitated.

"I'll send provisions with you, then. Let it not be said that I am unreasonable." The witch pushed back her chair and rose. "I suggest you set out at once, as it will take you several days to reach your destination."

"How will I find it?" Adelinde tried not to sound hopeless.

The northern forests were both vast and largely uninhabited after the fall of the kingdom to the north. Fear of the dragon kept people clustered near the capital, where the presence of the king's armies offered the illusion of safety. She did not fear the wilderness, but she did not know how to navigate it, either.

"Travel northwest. Eventually, you'll find the old road, and the markers should still be there." Heldin motioned toward the door as she rounded her desk.

Adelinde stepped back until she was in the dark room she'd passed through before. The witch slid past her and she trailed along behind as the woman led the way through the house and into a cozy kitchen. Cabinets and pantries opened themselves to expose the foodstuffs hidden inside.

"I would suggest one more thing, too." Heldin took a basket from the floor and began to fill it, the way a mother might prepare a picnic.

"For the trip?" Adelinde asked.

"For safety," the witch replied. "Leave the prince here, lest he be devoured by something in the woods. A glass bottle serves well to carry him, but is really no protection at all."

Adelinde held the bottle a little tighter while she considered. It made sense; she didn't disagree. She'd been frightened enough when Aldram tapped at the glass, trying to see what was inside. Her heart ached at the thought, though, and her throat grew tight. To leave him with Heldin struck her as wrong, as if it meant the woman was to be trusted. Yet as the witch extended her hand, she couldn't think of any better options. He was safest there, staying in one place, with someone who desperately needed him. His needs would be seen to, because without a prince, the witch had no schemes.

She gave the bottle to the witch and prayed it was not betrayal.

When Adelinde reached the forest stream again, she carried only the wicker basket. She stopped at the edge of the water and scanned the trees, but it was still dark, and their leaves blotted out the stars.

"That doesn't look like your sweetheart," Aldram said from somewhere overhead.

She managed not to jump. "I left him."

"With the witch?" the crow asked, incredulous.

"She needs him made human again. He's safer staying there than if I carry him everywhere we need to go." Adelinde didn't know why she was defending herself. It wasn't as if Bastian's fate mattered to the bird.

He fluttered down to land on her shoulder. She was prepared for it this time, though his claws still scratched. "So you've got an assignment? Best we get started, then. What did she ask for?"

"Wyrmstooth lilies." She didn't know which direction was north, and she turned a slow circle as she tried to gain her bearings based on the way they'd come.

"Strange choice for fixing a curse," Aldram murmured. "But I suppose she'll know her magic best of all. I won't pretend to know how witches work. Hard to find, though. They were more plentiful up north, before the razing happened."

She chose a direction, still unsure of where they should go, and pressed into the woods. "You've seen them before?"

The crow bobbed his head. "You see a lot of things, winging around the forests. And the witch travels widely. Turn that way, girly. You're pointed back toward the capital now."

Adelinde turned as he'd instructed. "She said we could find some at an old church up north. Near the border. Is that where we're headed now?"

"More or less. I don't know about churches, but I suppose that could be what the old ruin I'm thinking of was. A lot's fallen down, you know. Along the border and farther north." He settled low on her shoulder, his feathers warm against her skin.

"A lot will fall down here, if we don't do something about this curse." She didn't mean to grumble, but it was hard not to. She could not help but curse Bastian's stubbornness. What good would it do to marry her if the dragon might kill them both?

"Well, no worries, girly. I know just where we need to go. I've been all over this forest, I know it as well as..." He trailed off and flexed one wing, examining it as the stiff feathers dragged across the top of her sleeve. "Hmm. I suppose I can't say that anymore, can I? Haven't got any hands. Well, I did, once. Nice, strong ones, with callused palms and hair on the knuckles. I can picture that as well as where we need to go, so that's good enough."

She crinkled her nose. "If you say so."

"What, do you doubt me?" Aldram sounded wounded.

"You're a talking bird and you haven't given me a lot of reasons to believe anything you've said about the witch and your curse," she said.

"But you're going the direction I suggested."

"I haven't got many choices."

"And I did get you to the witch's house, didn't I?" He nudged her cheek with one wing, a gesture much like a friendly elbowing. "I'm not sure what else you could want to prove my sincerity. We're obviously both dealing with curses, here. Me just a little more personally than you."

Adelinde cast him a suspicious side-eye. "How did you come to be cursed, anyway?"

He sidestepped, putting himself farther down the slope of her shoulder. "Oh, now that is a very personal question. Very personal indeed, and I'd rather not discuss that with a stranger."

"Was it greed?" she guessed.

He gave a rasping croak, clearly offended. "Certainly not."

She smirked. "Was it a girl, then?"

The crow did not reply right away. Instead, he put his head down, and if his face had been able to show emotion, his sorrow would have been deep. "It's always matters of the heart, isn't it?"

Adelinde sobered. "And she didn't rescue you?"

"She couldn't," Aldram said. "We'll leave it at that."

She chose not to press further and merely let the bird guide her through the woods.

Near dawn, she'd grown so tired that she began to stumble, and Aldram left her shoulder to lead the way to a small clearing.

"You'll need to rest before we move on," he announced as he found a good perch and stopped. "Settle and sleep for a while. I'll keep watch."

She was too tired to argue. "If you let something devour me, neither one of us is doing any curse-breaking."

"The night's creatures are retiring and the day brings safety. Don't worry, girly. You're safe as can be until we get there."

She was exhausted, and the morning sun that dappled the ground where she settled brought a soothing warmth to her skin. The way he'd said that was odd, but she decided not to question and let sleep take her instead.

Several days into their trek, Aldram's meaning became clear.

"That must be the church," Adelinde whispered as she peered at the ruin below. The hill upon which they'd emerged was a good vantage point, but seeing what awaited them brought no comfort. Exploring ruins to find an old garden was one thing.

Exploring ruins inhabited by brigands was another.

"Looks like a dozen, give or take," Aldram said. "Weren't so many the last time I was here. Just looters, back then, since it wasn't long after good old Athanor was razed."

Adelinde frowned at him. "That was years ago. You haven't been this far north in all that time?"

"What does that matter? I've got a memory like a vise and a sense of direction that even a lodestone would envy. Besides, I got us here. I'll think of something to get us back, too." The crow examined the scene below as he spoke.

She couldn't help but watch him, instead of paying attention to the brigands at work in the ruin. Aldram didn't move like a bird; his movement was soft and fluid, rather than the quick, twitching motions of a mere animal. It was eerie, thick with a sense of something that wasn't quite right, but she already knew what he was and the oddity gave her no fear. Instead, it made her think of the way Bastian had stretched up the walls of the potion bottle as a worm, and she couldn't help the wave of sorrow that took her as she envisioned him reaching for her.

Eventually, Aldram took notice. "Your eyes will be more useful if they stay on the job." He flicked his head toward the ruin. "If I wanted to be stared at, I'd take a job doing tricks in the town square."

"Your tongue's as sharp as your beak, isn't it?" Adelinde murmured.

He batted his wings and pecked her fingers.

She jerked back her hand and sucked in a breath.

"We're going down there," Aldram said. "I'll see what I can do to cause a ruckus, you find that flower. The garden should be around the back." He hopped forward and spread his wings to take flight.

Adelinde grabbed him by the tail. "Wait! What if they see me?"

"Then you'd better hike up your skirts and run, because even with a sword in my hand, I'd be hard pressed to fight off a dozen men at once. And I haven't got hands." Aldram wiggled his wingtips at her.

Reluctantly, she let go, lest he peck her hand again. "Maybe you should just fetch the flowers, yourself."

The crow scoffed. "Now, what did I just say? How am I supposed to pick flowers without any fingers? You quit your bellyaching and be ready to move as soon as I stir things up."

"Fine," Adelinde sighed as Aldram departed. She inched back from the hill's peak and stood, unsure what she was supposed to be watching for. The men below were moving crates and sorting their contents, and none of them noticed as the bird flew into the structure that had once been the church's sanctuary.

It was not long before a crash sounded, followed by angry shouts and loud, strident cawing. The men outside abandoned their work and hurried inside.

That was her chance.

Adelinde sprinted down the hillside with her skirts hiked up around her calves and prayed the next task the witch had for her would give her a chance to change into more sensible clothing.

She darted around the back of the old church and froze when she saw the garden. A thorny tangle of overgrown flowers greeted her, and there were no lilies in sight.

Determined, she shoved the brambles out of the way and sought the mossy stones of the garden's walkway with her toes. They were hard to find beneath the weeds, but she pressed on past the thorns that snared her dress and tore the fine silk threads, unwilling to quit when the task was so simple.

Something white flashed between the gnarled witches'

broom leaves of unkempt roses. Adelinde elbowed a branch aside and her breath caught when the lilies came into view.

They were real. They looked just like the illustrations in her mother's herbal tomes, the long, curled white petals streaked with red.

"Wyrmstooth," Adelinde breathed. Several of the plants stood along the back wall of the church, their blossoms turned toward the sky. More than enough to meet the witch's needs.

More than enough to save Bastian.

She winced as thorns scratched and scraped welts into her skin, but she didn't have to lean far for the stems of the lilies to be within reach. She snagged one and twisted and the plant tore out of the earth, roots and all. Good. It would be easier to keep the flowers in good condition with the root ball attached.

On the other side of the stone wall, a loud crash and angry bellow made her cringe. How long could Aldram distract them? She held the flower high overhead and worked to twist herself free of the thorny brambles. Thin lines of crimson crisscrossed over her exposed arms and she dared not think of the scratches hidden underneath the gown. Threads on her dress caught and she pulled until the fabric ripped. She grimaced at the noise, but while it was loud to her ears, the cacophony the bird caused inside all but drowned it out.

She stumbled free of the overgrowth and gasped when she almost fell.

"Get moving!" Aldram barked from the top of the wall.

Adelinde glanced back just in time to see him dive back into the room below, but she did not stop. Freed from the thorns, she ran for the woods with all the strength and speed she could muster.

She did not stop when she reached the trees, nor did she stop when Aldram appeared beside her, winging between the trunks.

"That's it," he said, reassuring and encouraging, though he never turned his head her way. He outpaced her before long and she pushed herself to pursue him into the thick of the woods with the lily plant cradled close against her chest.

Eventually, her legs ached and her breath scorched so hot in her lungs that she stumbled to a stop and thought she might collapse.

"Oh, I've done something stupid," she gasped between breaths.

"Hold yourself steady, breathe in through your nose, deep as you can." The crow circled back to land beside her. "What have you done?"

She tried to breathe the way he instructed, but it still felt as if she couldn't get enough air. She gulped and answered anyway. "I left the basket. With all the food."

He gave her a flat stare. "That's it?"

"All our supplies were in there." Even the water skin the witch had provided for the trip had been in that basket.

"Well, luckily for you, you're in a lush forest with a creature that might know a thing or two about foraging." He eyed the plant she still held. "Suppose we ought to wet those roots and get a move on. I don't think those louts followed us, but it's best if we stay on the move."

Adelinde was grateful for that. "Who are they?"

"Scavengers. Thieves. Smugglers. Who knows. A lot of them out here in the woods, ever since Athanor fell." He couldn't shrug, but he moved his wings in an approximation. "Come along. There should be a stream not far from here with water clean enough to drink. You can finish catching your breath there."

"And what if they come after us?" She looked back, but saw nothing other than trees.

Aldram launched himself into the branches and began to lead the way. "Then hopefully you'll have caught your breath and will be fresh enough to run some more. But honestly, what reason do they have to follow us? I doubt a smuggling outfit would care much about you taking a flower from an old garden."

Perhaps that was true. Even a flower as rare as wyrmstooth was nothing but pretty to most. She shuffled after him, her feet and legs leaden from fatigue. Her hips and knees ached, but she could not afford to give in to their protests now. "Then what was the need for a distraction?"

He paused on a branch and peered down at her. "Can't say I'd feel right about letting a girl walk into a nest of ruffians all by herself. Maybe it would be nothing. Maybe they'd just tell you to pick your flowers and go on. Or maybe... maybe you'd be the next treasure they'd cart out of here."

Heat rose in her cheeks and Adelinde dropped her gaze to the forest ahead. "Oh."

"But it's behind us now," the crow added, as if to reassure her. "I suspect Heldin knew that possibility, and things didn't go as she planned. With fortune, the rest of your tasks will be as clean and easy as this one."

She regarded the scratches and cuts on her hands and forearms and was not sure that description was accurate, but it could have been much worse. "The hard part must be what's ahead."

"The other tasks?"

Adelinde shook her head. "Cooperating with the witch."

"Ah." Aldram chuckled. "Well, best steel yourself then, girly. There's no escaping that."

She hated that he was right.

Six

The brigands in the church did not pursue them. Adelinde was grateful; the return trip was difficult enough without conflict. Aldram scouted for water and food and turned up enough to keep both their bellies full, but when he was foraging, he could not guide the way, and so the going was slow.

"We're getting close now," Aldram announced as he perched in the latest bush he'd found and helped himself to the summer berries. "Hope old Heldin is happy to see you. I suspect she thought it would be easier to be rid of you than this."

"If she gets rid of me, she has to gather all the reagents for her magic by herself." Adelinde settled beside the bush to pick her own meal. She was not used to so much walking and a moment's rest was appreciated.

"If I'm being honest, I don't think she's after reagents," the crow said.

She frowned at him, then turned her attention to the lilies as she put them down. She'd torn a piece from her underskirt to wrap the root ball and keep it moist, and the flowers had adapted well, though their petals had become bruised. "What makes you say that?"

"Wyrmstooth is a toxic flower. You know that, don't you?" He paused to eat and ruffled his feathers. "You wouldn't be a very good herbalist if you didn't."

"What does that matter? Hemlock is a deadly poison too, but also a potent medicine. Many dangerous things can be beneficial if used correctly." And the remedy the witch would provide for Bastian was magic, besides. Adelinde's specialty was medicine; her expertise only went so far. "She must know something I don't, that's all."

The crow side eyed her.

It made her shoulders bunch. "What's that look for?"

"I think you know more than you're letting on, that's what. You're the one who came running out into the woods with your sweetheart in a potion bottle. There's a bit of magic in you, too, isn't there?"

Adelinde blinked at him, taken aback. "What?"

"Herbalists mix teas and tinctures. They don't tote around bottles for that sort of brew. How'd you get it, if not pouring out something you mixed up?" Aldram flicked his beak skyward in challenge.

Heat crept into her cheeks and she lowered her eyes. "It was a love potion. For Bastian."

"So you started all this on purpose?" Aldram asked incredulously.

"No," she snapped. "It was supposed to help him, for when he proposed to the witch's daughter."

He hopped to a closer branch and hunched forward to meet her at eye level. "Love potions aren't medicine, girly."

"I know." She couldn't keep the desperation from her voice. "I know I shouldn't have. I just thought... It was supposed to make things easier. For him." She'd always known it wouldn't make anything easier for her. She was still losing him. Even if she managed to rescue him now, that wouldn't change.

"But you admit it, then. A bit of magic in the old veins." His voice dropped to a whisper, the gleam in his eye something more than just interest.

Adelinde sobered. "I'm not a witch."

The crow snickered. "Never said you were, girly. But that's an interesting thing to know. Now we'll just have to see if it does you any favors." He launched himself out of the bush and winged up to a nearby tree. "Get yourself a snack for the walk, then come along. We've got more work to do."

She plucked another handful of berries and pushed herself up, then retrieved the lilies from the ground. "What do you know about magic?" She shouldn't have encouraged him, yet she couldn't resist asking.

"A fair bit. More than I'd like, given my circumstances." Aldram never went more than a few trees ahead. "Enough to know there are different sorts. There are those that bite and those that bless. I'm just unfortunate enough to have more experience with the first."

"Does that worry you?" She ducked under a branch to follow.

"What, the biting? I don't think you've got it in you. Besides, it's not as if you're unique. Plenty of folk with a bit of the old magic in them, especially up north. Athanor was full of them. Most just never figure out how to use it." He made an odd sound, almost a cluck, and came to an easy stop a bit farther away.

Adelinde frowned more. Little was said about the people of Athanor; after the dragon's arrival and the fall of the northern kingdom, people avoided speaking of the place as if doing so might draw the dragon's attention. Some believed it had, that a refusal to let the beast take the north without question was what had drawn it southward, toward Ceresia. That the bird spoke so freely was odd.

"Are you from Athanor?" she asked.

"Are you? Or your parents, maybe?" Aldram turned toward her, but did not fly any farther.

She crested the hill and the witch's estate came into view. "No. At least, I don't think so."

"Well, your loss. It was a beautiful place. Before all the fire and destruction, that is." He flicked his wings and jerked his beak toward the mansion. "Go on, then. I can't go any farther than this without her feeling that I'm here, and that's a whole kettle of fish on its own. I'll be waiting for you when you set out for the next task."

If there was a next task. She hadn't forgotten the suggestion that the witch had meant to kill her, rather than have her obtain the lilies, and there was no guarantee the next errand would be any safer. "Thank you," she said, all the same.

Adelinde held the flowers close as she picked her way through the woods to the stone house. All the while, she tried not to marvel. It was a beautiful place, and far more welcoming than it had been in the dark. Birdsong carried on the wind and flowers in the witch's garden perfumed the air. As she strode past the gardens, Adelinde couldn't help but look to see if it held any wyrmstooth lilies. She did not know if their absence was a relief.

The door did not open when she approached. She stood in front of it for a moment before she gathered the will to knock. Half of her expected the witch's magic would answer when she did, but instead, the door creaked open to reveal a figure on the other side.

Adelinde's breath hitched.

Florina.

The witch's daughter gave her a curious look, and Adelinde silently cursed herself.

Of course the witch's daughter was there; she lived there with her mother. But while she hadn't expected to see the young woman, she had expected Florina would be more put-together. The person before her now was weary, dressed in plain clothes with a stained apron, her flaxen hair a mess in its bun and her eyes red and swollen. Whether it was exhaustion or tears that had made them that way, Adelinde didn't know.

"I've brought the wyrmstooth lilies I was asked for." She presented the travel-bruised flowers as confidently as she could and decided to pretend she didn't recognize who stood before her. "Could you please let Lady Heldin know I've arrived?"

Florina scarcely opened her mouth to speak before the door snapped open wide.

"Come," the witch's voice boomed, though there was no one else in the entryway.

"I'll take you to her study." Florina stepped aside and motioned for her to enter.

"Thank you." Adelinde slipped in beside her, her eyes fixed on the way her tattered and stained ballgown swirled around her ankles. She didn't want to look at the young woman who turned to escort her through the place, didn't want the vision of her with Bastian to plague her as she worked to set him free.

Together, in silence, they retraced the same path Adelinde had taken alone before.

Did Florina know what she was doing? Were her eyes red from tears over Bastian, or over how what had been intended as her engagement party had gone so terribly wrong? Adelinde resented her existence, yet she couldn't help but pity her. Nothing had gone according to her plans, either.

When they reached the witch's study, little about the room resembled what Adelinde had seen before. The bookshelves and large desk remained, but the books, papers, and scrolls had been meticulously organized. Instead of study materials, a variety of bottles and jars cluttered the desk, and a cabinet containing more of such supplies stood open behind the witch.

Heldin scarcely looked up from the book in her hands as she paced back and forth behind her desk. Florina stopped in the doorway and Adelinde paused at her side. A long moment of weighted silence passed before the witch seemed to realize they were there.

"You've returned," Heldin said, her surprise as clear as the way she stared at the flowers in Adelinde's hands.

"With three wyrmstooth lilies, as you required," Adelinde replied.

A faint crinkle formed between the older woman's brows. "And so swiftly."

"They were just where you said they would be, in the garden of an abandoned church near the border. Without your direction, it would have been much harder to find, my lady." Adelinde curtsied and the lilies bobbed with her.

Heldin pursed her lips, then beckoned her with one finger. "Bring it here, child. Pluck the three flowers and lay them with the rest of my reagents, then give the roots to my daughter. That will make a fine addition to my garden."

Adelinde hurried forward and lowered the root ball to the edge of the desk. The moment her hands were free, she steadied the plant and snapped the flowers from their stems. One by one, she laid them on the desk between bottles of herbs and a bowl of small animal bones. Her eyes traveled from one container to another.

"Looking for your sweetheart?" Heldin asked with an edge of mockery in her voice. "He's over there, on the shelf." She flicked her fingers that way, not direction, not dismissal.

"May I see him?" Adelinde let go of the last flower and stepped back with the plant's root ball in her hands. Florina reached for it, and she let her take it without a second glance.

"For a moment. Then you will need to set off for the next reagent, hmm?" There was no warmth in the witch's smile.

Adelinde considered staying put, but her gaze drifted to the shelf and she could not make herself look away. It was easier if she did not acknowledge him that way. If she pretended he was whole and well and simply hidden. But it was not the truth, and she could not resist slipping across the witch's study to see the bottle that had become his prison.

Dirt and moss now filled the lower half of the glass bottle, and though she looked at it from every angle she could without touching it, she saw no sign of Bastian's new form. "I can't see him."

"Of course not. He's a worm." Heldin almost snickered. "He's buried himself and has been quite comfortable. Later, I may even give him some apple peelings to eat. Rest assured, child, your beloved is quite happy."

Adelinde hoped that was true. She gave the bottle one last wistful glance, then trudged back to the witch's desk. "What do you need from me next?" With all the herbs that sat out, part of her hoped the next step was brewing something. That, she at least knew something about.

"So eager for your second task. Very well, there's no reason to keep you here. The next thing you retrieve may prove more difficult." The witch plucked each petal from the wyrmstooth lilies and dropped them into an empty mortar. "Bring me a song."

"A song?" Adelinde repeated, unsure she'd heard correctly.

"Yes. The song of an enchanted nightingale. Not all magic comes from mixing potions, little girl." This time, when Heldin smiled at her, there was no doubt it was malicious.

The name of the bird put a lump of uneasiness in her belly and Adelinde fought to ignore it. It had to be a coincidence; the witch couldn't have known Bastian's pet name for her. "Where am I supposed to find something like that?" Never mind capturing it to bring it back.

Heldin scoffed. "If I had all the answers, I would have everything I needed right here and wouldn't need an errand girl. Go find it and bring it back here, and be quick about it."

Adelinde's jaw tightened, but she didn't dare protest. Instead, she shuffled backwards and gave a curtsy before she excused herself from the grand house.

An enchanted nightingale. She scarcely knew where to begin. Weariness fell over her shoulders like a mantle and she bowed her head to scrub her face with both hands as she trudged along the well-worn dirt path.

"Go north."

Adelinde stopped, startled, and turned this way and that before she spotted Florina in the garden.

The other girl held a shovel with both hands, her face made hollow by the purple circles beneath her eyes. She smiled, though weakly, and rubbed her forehead with the back of her wrist. "To fetch what my mother wants."

"Why should you help me?" Adelinde didn't mean for it to sound sulky; she flinched at the sullen sound of her own voice.

Florina gave the smallest shrug and twisted her hands around the shovel's timeworn handle. "I want him changed back, too."

Of course she did. She was the one who had been promised the prince's hand.

But Florina turned back to her work without argument or complaint, occupied with digging a hole for the wrapped lily plant on the ground beside her feet. "All the answers you need will be to the north. That is all I'll say. Good luck, miss..."

"Adelinde," she provided. For all that they'd seen each other a dozen times, she'd never spoken to the witch's daughter. Not directly.

"I'm Florina."

The need for an introduction made her more human, less of a faceless enemy, and Adelinde couldn't say she appreciated the way it felt. "Yes, I know."

"He's spoken of you every time we've met," Florina continued, though she didn't look up from her work. "I thought it was you, but it's nice to finally connect your name and face in my mind."

Adelinde would have preferred to stay out of the girl's thoughts altogether. "Thank you for the directions. Please make sure Bastian is looked after while I am gone."

"I will," Florina said with a sweet smile. "And after."

There had been no unkindness in those words, but they struck Adelinde as such a jab that her hackles rose. She gave a curt nod of farewell to the witch's daughter and headed north— not because the girl had told her to, but because it was where Aldram waited. If more travel lay ahead, there were more preparations to make, and Adelinde would not be caught unprepared again.

Seven

"Well, that's sure not one I've heard before." Aldram hunched low on Adelinde's shoulder as she trudged back toward the village. South of the palace, some parts of the forest were familiar enough she did not need the crow's guidance, and from the path he'd led her to after their departure from the witch's estate, the tips of the palace's towers were visible above the trees. It would be easy to reach home from there.

"So do you think we should go north, like Florina said? Or should we try something else?" A sense of urgency still hung about Adelinde's shoulders like a cloak, but she knew she could not travel any farther in the tattered gown she still wore. She plotted a path through the woods in her head, ensuring she'd be able to reach the village without anyone seeing her in such a state.

The crow gave a soft hum. "I'll think on it. Maybe something will come to mind. I am a bird, though, and I can't say I've met any nightingales."

"At least not any cursed ones, right?" She tilted her head to look at him as she walked. Her joints protested and her limbs ached, but she tried to keep a steady pace. Every inch of her would be more comfortable once she had a chance to dress properly for the trip.

"None at all, I'm afraid. I don't interact much with songbirds. They tend to be afraid of me. As if poor old Aldram is frightening." He raised a wing to his head, the same way he might have pressed the back of one hand to his forehead in dramatic despair.

"Well, songbirds aren't fond of crows," Adelinde said, though she wasn't sure it would make him feel better. "Are there many people cursed the way you are?"

"To be birds? Not that I've seen. One or two, through the years, though it's usually the girls who go and get themselves in this sort of mess. Sort of funny that you'd end up helping two cursed blokes, instead of you being the cursed one."

She tried to smile. "Hopefully I'll be able to rescue at least one of you, then. I have a question, though. She asked for an enchanted nightingale, not a cursed one. You say you don't know any cursed birds, but what about those? They are different, aren't they?"

"Oh, leagues different. Remember what I said before, girly? About magic that bites and magic that blesses? It's a perfect example, right there. Curses are an affliction, laid on you to hurt. Enchantment is a blessing. It gives something, instead of taking something away." He nodded as he spoke, as if he was an expert on the subject.

Adelinde supposed he was. He knew far more about magic than she ever would, having been a firsthand victim of the witch's power. "Are enchanted birds just regular birds with a blessing of magic, then?"

"More or less. There could be any number of them out there in those woods, but to find a nightingale, you'll need to go where they can be found all the time. Birds of a feather, or so they say. They'll want to be near their own kind. Just like the two of us flock together, stuck dealing with these curses, eh?" His wing nudged her cheek, eliciting the smallest smile.

It wasn't funny, being stuck working with the black bird perched on her shoulder, but she found herself grateful for his presence. If it weren't for him, she would still be looking for the witch's estate.

"At least I'm not alone."

Aldram gave a soft chuckle, then cleared his throat. She'd never heard such a strange noise; it wasn't quite the same as when a man did it, and the hoarse scraping of his body's natural voice made her skin rise in gooseflesh.

"Sorry," he murmured. "Ah, I meant to ask, were you planning to head north? Because I know you asked for a road, but you're going the wrong direction."

"On purpose." She plucked at her skirt with both hands, the silk limp and tattered. "I can't keep running around the forest dressed like this."

The crow cocked his head and looked down at her dress. "Well, you could, but I suppose there are more practical things to wear. Trousers, if you've got them. I hear that's fashionable down south. Haven't been that far, myself, but the other birds have told me all about it."

"You can speak to regular birds?" The possibility had never crossed her mind.

"Some. I wish they'd shut up, if I'm honest."

Perhaps that was the solution for finding the next road they should take. "Do you think you could ask them where we might find nightingales? I'll make my way back to my cottage to dress and pack supplies for the trip. Perhaps you could find out and meet me there?"

Aldram offered a skeptical hum in response. "I suppose I could try."

"If you do, it'll get both of us that much closer to being done with the witch." Adelinde doubted he needed any incentive beyond that, but she still hoped he didn't ask for any. They were supposed to be cooperating to find the answers. That was as far as their deal had gone.

Eventually, the crow heaved a sigh, his wings and tail drooping against her shoulder as he threatened to deflate. "All right, I'll give it my best. Just be warned, birdsong's not the sweet serenade people seem to think. Most of what they have to say isn't very pleasant at all, but I'll subject myself to it for you."

Her face brightened. "Thank you, Aldram. I'll have some nice, ripe berries waiting for you when you find my cottage."

He couldn't roll his eyes, so his whole head rocked, instead. "Don't think you can bribe me, girly. The herbalist's shack at the edge of the woods, is it?"

Part of her was surprised he knew, but it made sense that he might. If he'd been following Heldin, he'd likely been all over Ceresia... and Athanor, too, by his own claims. "Yes, that's the one."

"Then I'll see you there. Be careful, girly. We don't have long before the witch will have an eye on you."

Before Adelinde had a chance to ask what he meant, Aldram leaped off her shoulder and disappeared into the trees, leaving her with a sinking weight in the pit of her stomach.

Would Heldin try to watch her? The witch hadn't seemed to have known about anything that happened with the wyrmstooth lilies, and if there was a potion to be made, the woman would have her hands full.

Then again, Aldram's suspicion the lilies hadn't been a reagent, so much as an effort to get rid of her, sprang to mind. If that truly had been the goal, then the witch would be disappointed it had failed, in which case the possibility she might have Heldin's attention became more real.

A prickle of uneasiness ran up the back of Adelinde's neck and she did her best to shake it free and march on. No; if that was the case, and if Aldram truly wanted to avoid the witch's attention—as he'd claimed whenever they neared her house— then he wouldn't have chosen to ride about on her shoulder while she made her way home.

With that small sliver of comfort fixed in the forefront of her mind, Adelinde breathed easier, and the hours it took to reach her home at the forest's edge passed in peace.

It was early evening when she reached the cottage, and the rosy glow of the sun's fading light made the place all the more charming. She lingered outside for a moment, a knot wedging itself in her throat.

Home had always been a comfort. She'd spent so many days working in that garden with her mother, and then more days alone, after her mother's spirit had been called from life. The flowers and herbs were just as tidy as when she'd departed, yet now, their bright blossoms and vibrant leaves held no cheer and brought her no peace.

How many times had Bastian stood among the flowers so he could lean in her window and talk to her while she worked? She had known which visit would be the last, but seeing that worn patch of dirt right beneath the window was different now. Knowing he would never stand there again, even if her quest succeeded.

The plants would grow back, the gap would fill, but the growth of the garden would never fill the hollow his absence would carve into her heart.

"But he still needs you," she whispered to herself.

She made herself walk, forced her fingers to curl around the latch on the door. It stuck when she pulled, as usual, and she jostled the latch until it let go. She'd always meant to have someone look at it, but it had been unimportant. Now it was another unpleasant reminder of how unwelcoming her return to that cottage would be.

Adelinde shook her head as she stepped inside. "But you don't have time to sulk." Aldram was fast on his wings, and she needed to be ready to leave the moment he returned with information.

The first order was getting out of her dress. She struggled to unfasten the bodice on her own, but her arms bent farther at the shoulder and elbow than they probably ought, and her fingertips found what they needed with a little concentration. When everything was said and done, perhaps she could salvage some of the silk. For now, she satisfied herself with draping the ruined gown over the top of her dressing screen with a silent promise she wouldn't leave it forgotten.

There had been no fire on the hearth, so there was no warm water, but a quick wash in something cold restored vigor to her limbs. Adelinde did not own many clothes, but she did have an old pair of comfortable trousers that were suitable for travel, so she donned them with a simple blouse and found her good boots under the bed.

Last of all, she retrieved her rings from the wooden box on her bedside table.

They had been the finest gift Bastian had ever given her, aside from his presence in her life. Her joints had bothered her less when she'd been a child, but she hadn't been responsible for so much work then. After her mother's passing, she had taken over the hard work of picking and grinding herbs, and that was when she'd first noticed how terrible the pain of her loose joints could be.

But Bastian had noticed.

He'd seen the way she struggled on her bad days, how she would shake her hands or rub her joints when her fingers became stuck. He'd studied the way her knuckles bent too far in the wrong directions, and he'd commissioned her jewelry the next day.

Each of the gold rings she slid onto her fingers had been shaped just for her, based on how her hands moved—and how they shouldn't. The connected bands held each joint in place, lending her fingers extra strength. Her hands clinked as she flexed them, and the rings settled in place. The sound had always been a pleasant reminder of him. Of the fact he cared.

Now, they would remind her of what she fought to save.

The last thing to do was to pack for the trip, though she still did not know where they were going. She had all but finished filling a satchel with supplies before a flutter of wings announced Aldram's arrival at the windowsill above her work table.

"About ready, are you?" He hopped onto the work table, casting a curious glance toward the loose fragment of herbs scattered across its surface. "Well, glad as I am to see you dedicated to the cause, I'm going to suggest you slow down and rest, first."

Adelinde paused with her hand still inside the bag. "Did you learn something?"

He nodded, though she took the notion he would have preferred to shrug. "Got a bit of a lead for us, though I'm afraid it's also bad news."

Slowly, she withdrew her hand from the satchel and folded its top closed. "Well, where are we going?"

Aldram sighed and turned his beak toward the ceiling. "North," he said, as if it pained him. "All the way to the heart of Athanor."

So Florina had been right. "What's wrong with that?" She knew it was a long way to travel, but if they took what had once been major roads, the trip would not be difficult.

"Think for a second, girly." Aldram hopped to the edge of the table and lowered his head. His feathers ruffled, gleaming in the soft candlelight. "What might one find in the middle of Athanor?"

"The capital," Adelinde replied slowly.

"And what's *in* the capital, to keep everyone else out?"

Understanding lit in her like a fire and her heart sank.

The witch really was trying to kill her.

Eight

"For the last time, I'm not turning back." Adelinde worked to temper her frustration as she gave the same answer she'd given every other time Aldram asked, but she couldn't keep it from bleeding through into her voice.

The crow ducked his head. "All right. I'm just saying there would be no shame in it, that's all."

They were already three days deep into travel, and though they weren't the only ones on the road, they were the only ones headed north.

Folk from all over upper Ceresia filtered onto the road with wagons and livestock in tow, most solemn, many fearful. Whispers of Prince Bastian's disappearance had filtered across the country in the week since the ball, and everyone who traveled had reached the same conclusion: that, in the absence of a royal wedding, there would be no help in fighting the dragon.

Adelinde could scarcely believe it had already been so long. Nor could she believe the rumors shared by people who had stopped to speak with her as she walked.

Prince Bastian had fled, some claimed, forsaking his country.

Others claimed he had died, having been poisoned by a jaded lover.

Those rumors bothered her most. They had to be spawned by her presence, by what partygoers had seen—her trying to push the potion she'd made into Bastian's hands, just before the witch's magic struck.

She tried to keep her head up and remain confident as conversation lulled and they passed another cluster of weary-eyed travelers. Aldram kept quiet whenever there were people close by, and she'd decided that was probably best. The last thing she needed was for people to mistake *her* for a witch, with a talking crow perched on her shoulder. They gave the black bird enough distrustful looks as it was.

Eventually, he craned his neck to look behind them and concluded they'd gone far enough from the latest bunch for him to speak again. "There were more people in the northern bits of the kingdom than I realized. Can't help but wonder how many were refugees from Athanor."

Adelinde assumed that was most of them. Athanor had been an ally, and when the kingdom fell to the dragon, many of the country's residents had taken shelter within Ceresia's borders. A fair number had fled further after Erich was slain, convinced that Ceresia was not safe, either.

"Do you think Heldin will really be able to stop the dragon?" She kept her voice low, despite the distance between them and the people they'd passed.

Aldram did not reply right away.

She shrugged twice, as if it might jostle an answer from him.

It worked.

"I think the dragon will stop when she gets what she wants, yes. It's just that I don't know what she's after. Not really." He stared ahead, but his dark eyes held a distant look. "What I think doesn't matter much, though. I'm just a bird."

She shrugged again. "But you weren't always." He'd been quick to tell her that, right after they met. "You were a confident man, once."

That yielded a laugh. "Confident? Whatever gives you that notion?"

"You're very determined in the way you speak. A little bossy, despite being a bird." She cracked a smile. "But you also mentioned swords when we were at the ruins of that church, and you seemed more than confident in your ability to fight. A normal person wouldn't claim to be only *hard pressed* by the idea of fending off a dozen men at once."

"Ah, you got me." Aldram chuckled, but he stood a little straighter on her shoulder and his breast feathers fluffed with pride. "I was one of the best swordsmen in Athanor, once upon a time. Trained every day of my life, from the moment I was old enough to hold a stick in my hands." His wing flicked out and the way the longest feathers tilted made her think of fingers.

"How come you didn't fight the dragon, then?" She was only teasing, but he scoffed and tucked his wing close.

"Because I was already a bird by the time the beast showed up, that's why. I don't think it would have appeared at all if I hadn't been incapacitated. Earthworms are afraid of birds. Fire-breathing wyrms sure aren't."

He'd told her he'd been trapped as a bird for years, but having dates cemented in her mind stirred her pity. It had been almost ten years since Athanor's fall. "That's a long time to be stuck that way."

"And a long time to be following that witch around, trying to figure out how it can be fixed," he agreed.

Adelinde nibbled at her lower lip as she considered her next question. They weren't exactly friends, not yet, and she didn't know how much he might let her pry. "And the girl you did this for, she didn't try to help change you back at all?"

The crow sobered and glanced away. "She would have. I know that with every fiber in me. With every feather. If she could, she would have given anything to fix my mistakes, but..."

"Something stopped her?" she asked.

Had it not been for his beak, she wouldn't have noticed the

way his head dropped. As it was, it was little more than a hair's breadth, though his posture grew stiff. "She died."

A soft ache stirred in her breast. "I'm so sorry."

"Ah, I knew it was possible," he muttered. He stared into the forest, distant and resigned. "That was what got me tangled up with Heldin to begin with, truth be told. I'd tried everything, everything to save her, and... well, when you've exhausted every other option, even a bitter old sorceress begins to look like help."

"And she cursed you? Instead of helping?" Adelinde could scarcely believe it. Even considering the witch's temper, that was extreme.

"Oh, she helped. It was a miracle, really. Whatever brew she mixed up for my girl fixed her, right as rain, and we were happy for a while. But it didn't last. The witch came back. She raised her price. I thought since she'd cured her with a potion, there was no going back." Aldram shook his head, and his regret was so thick that just seeing it made her chest grow tight.

And it planted seeds of fear, too.

What if Heldin went back on her word to help Bastian? What if everything she was doing was in vain? "She took the healing back?"

"Oh, no. I don't think even Heldin is powerful enough for that. But I refused to pay the new price, since it wasn't part of our deal. So Heldin made me into this, and my wife..." He sighed. "She never stood a chance."

So the witch had killed her.

Adelinde stayed silent.

After a time, Aldram sighed again and gave himself a shake. "There's no sense moping over it now, in any case. We've got a castle to get to and a dragon to get past. I don't suppose you've got any bright ideas?"

"Me? I thought you were the one with ideas. Can't you just distract the dragon while I look for the bird?" She wanted to laugh, but it wouldn't come. Instead, the sound caught in her throat and grew into a knot that threatened to choke her. What hope did she have to evade a dragon in its own territory? She was doomed.

"Well, maybe I'll look for the bird, then. Not sure if it'll speak to me, but it'll certainly be easier for me to get close, and if I speak with it, maybe I can convince it to help us out."

"You stand a better chance of convincing it than I do." Adelinde had not yet considered how she was supposed to collect a bird's song, and having the bird itself along for the trip made the most sense. She had no desire to trap and cage the nightingale for her benefit, but if that was what the task required, she would.

"We'll try that first, then. Just find somewhere for you to hide, and I'll see if I can wing about and find that nightingale. I still don't recall seeing any when I lived there, but things have changed. Maybe they can be found there now." Aldram didn't sound convinced, but the way he tried to reassure her despite his own doubts warmed her heart.

"Thank you," Adelinde murmured. "You're a good friend."

The crow's head snapped toward her in surprise. "Friend?"

"Aren't you?" They'd traveled together for days by this point, united in a common goal. If not friends, at least they were allies.

Aldram scoffed. "A mentor, more like. I'm twice your age, girly, and don't you forget it. You'll get none of that teenage twittering from me."

The tightness in her throat abated and this time, she could not have stopped her laugh if she tried. "Very well, then, Mister Aldram. If that is your name at all."

She expected the bird to cackle, recalling their first conversation, but he gave a soft hum instead.

"You know, it's funny," he said. "I know who I am, who I've been, but my name... Ever since the witch cursed me, it's been sort of muddled in my head, like I can't get it out."

"So it's *not* Aldram," she teased. It wasn't a surprise. He'd never claimed it was his name; all he'd said was that was what she could call him. With his jest about the fae and names, she'd all but expected it was a bluff.

"No, but it's close enough, I think. Or, maybe not. Aldram. Hmm." The bird cocked his head to one side. "Aldram is close... but what is it, really?"

She left him to his musing and walked. Athanor's capital was still days ahead.

Nine

The landscape changed little as they walked. Adelinde had never ventured outside of Ceresia, nor had she asked questions of those who did, but from the way common folk spoke of other kingdoms, she'd always assumed they would be different.

Perhaps they had been, back when Athanor still stood. Now, all she saw as she trekked through the countryside was a forest like any other.

Hills rose and dipped just like they did back home, and the same crisp scent of pine touched the air. The similarities made her heart ache strangely, homesickness tangled up with familiarity and a growing undercurrent of dread.

If Athanor had been so similar to Ceresia, then should Ceresia fall, the distinction between the two would be forgotten —just some nameless, ill-remembered boundary that separated her homeland from its fallen ally. Even the ruins they had passed were no different from what she supposed Ceresia's cities might become. Wooden beams rotted or charred the same, no matter where houses were built, and the stone was no different in color from what had been used to build her cottage.

"It's strange, how familiar it all is," she told Aldram after they'd reached the outskirts of what had once been the capital. Not a single building remained standing, save the palace—and even that had fallen into ruin.

Adelinde had expected to see the dragon perched atop its towers, but their crumbling peaks were as abandoned as the rest of the countryside. The pale stone glowed in the bright of day, as white as the clouds in the deep blue sky.

"Not familiar to me at all, I'm afraid," the crow replied.

Nature had been swift to reclaim the ruins. There was little in the way of full-grown trees, but saplings and weeds had sprouted from seemingly every inch of the city. Wildflowers peppered the cobblestone streets and Adelinde resisted the urge to bend and smell them as she crept toward the palace.

Not far from the edge of the city, Aldram leaned close beside her ear and spoke in low tones meant for her alone. "We ought to find some cover. Somewhere for you to huddle and wait while I wing about and see what I can find."

"I want to help," she protested.

The crow gave his head a vigorous shake. "You're no help to anyone if you're dead, and the wyrm could be back at any time. I won't feel its magic until it's too close to do anything about it. By then, it'll have seen us, and it'll be too late."

"Magic?" Adelinde repeated with a frown.

"All creatures like that have it in them. Whether it's the good kind or bad helps you tell what sort of nature they have, and the dragon here is bad. Very, very bad. Trust me on that, dove. Now." He scanned the ruined city twice over before he pointed with a wing. "There. See it? There's part of an old guard tower still standing. The first floor, at least. That'll be a perfect place for you to hide."

She studied the tower with a regretful frown. She didn't want to hide, but she would not refuse the wisdom in doing so. "How long do you think you will be?"

"I'll do a circuit of the city and then check the old king's woods. If anywhere is a hospitable place for birds, it's there. I'll meet you back at the tower, so don't get any grand ideas." The crow thrust himself from her shoulder before she could object. He'd taken to doing that often. Adelinde bit her tongue to keep it still, lest she shout her opinion on the practice and draw unwanted attention. Her thoughts could wait.

By the time she reached the ruined tower, Aldram was long out of sight. The inside of the tower was mossy and weedy, like the rest of the city, but the stone walls were still strong. There was no door, so she slipped into the cool shadow of the tower's interior and shrugged her satchel from her shoulders. It made her shoulders ache, and she would have been lying if she said she didn't enjoy the idea of rest. Walking made her hips hurt, the satchel's weight made her shoulders hurt, and weariness made the rest of her hurt, too. Adelinde sat on the uneven stone floor and stretched out her legs in front of her. She could rest, work on relieving the strain in her aching muscles, and with luck, Aldram would find a nightingale he could persuade to assist them.

What did one ask of an enchanted bird? She mulled over the thought while she drew her toes in a circle to stretch her ankles. One by one, she worked her joints in different directions until they were soothed. If she didn't stretch, she would stiffen up overnight as she slept, and the return trip would be that much harder.

As if one day was all it would take to find the nightingale they needed and let them be on their way. She snorted at the thought.

"It's too bad *you* aren't magic," she muttered to herself. "You're Bastian's Nightingale, aren't you?"

He'd been the only person she sang for, and considering the pet name he'd given her, she'd long suspected he treasured that fact. She'd done it when they'd first rescued him, to soothe him while her mother prepared the ingredients for the remedy that had saved his life. After that, she always sang when she worked with her herbs, and he had leaned against the windowsill to listen with a dreamy smile on his face.

But songs wouldn't help her now. Sure, she had a pinch of power in her blood. Her mother had never explained its origin, but the little something extra they could work into herbs to make potions had been part of what kept their business going. Heldin's magic was so far removed from what she could do that Adelinde could not even fathom the difference.

How was a song from an enchanted bird supposed to help? How could the witch seize magic from something else and incorporate it into Bastian's remedy?

The notion was so strange, Adelinde found herself rubbing her brow with her fingertips. She was supposed to be stretching, preparing for the next leg of their journey. Getting caught up in memories and thoughts would help no one, but the thought of Bastian at her window clung in the forefront of her mind, so she held it there and used it as a reminder of why she was here.

A dark shadow passed over the tower, blotting out the sunlight. Out of reflex, Adelinde shuffled backwards across the floor until her shoulders brushed the wall. Harsh, ripping wingbeats tore at the air.

Adelinde had never seen the dragon. Few who had seen it had lived. Fear made her skin prickle, but curiosity made her itch. Descriptions had been scarce, and they varied so widely that she had only the simplest idea of what the beast might look like.

When the wingbeats passed, she shifted forward onto her hands and knees, then pressed herself up to her feet. The weeds underfoot muted the heels of her sturdy boots and, against her better judgment, she tiptoed along the wall until she reached the doorway and could look out.

None of the stories could have prepared her for what she saw.

The dragon was nearly the size of the castle itself. It landed atop the structure with a crash, the weight of its form sending fragments of walls tumbling to the ground. The stone crackled like thunder as it landed in the ruins of the palace below.

Fear clawed at Adelinde's heart like never before, twisting and tangling to fall into her belly like a lead weight.

That was the beast that had killed Bastian's brother, that had altered their fates and the directions of their lives forever. It raised its head, the many horns around its great black head tangled like the branches of a bramble. Its wings remained half-furled as it tilted its maw to the sky and gave a long, angry roar. The earth beneath Adelinde's feet trembled and her insides sank.

How had anyone ever believed they could slay it?

The dragon's long, whip-like tail snaked up and then thrashed like that of an agitated cat. Its head turned one way and then another, its movements slow and filled with purpose. The deliberate motion made her queasy.

It was looking for something.

Aldram. Adelinde's eyes darted in the direction her companion had flown, but he was long gone and the sky was empty. The city was empty, she realized with a start. Where there had been scurrying wildlife in the weeds and cheerful birdsong in the air at their arrival, there was now a weighty silence, as if the entire ruined city held its breath.

She held hers, too, and slid back into the shadows of the tower. Cold sweat made her shirt cling to the length of her spine and plastered her dark hair to the back of her neck.

Had the crow escaped notice? Surely he wasn't foolish enough to venture around the castle while the dragon was there. A normal bird might go ignored, but if he could sense magic in the dragon because of what had been done to him, surely the dragon would be able to sense him, too.

And it was looking for something. It rotated in place as it searched and the earth trembled as more of the ruined castle collapsed beneath its feet. Adelinde shrank farther back into the tower, away from the door, praying she hadn't been seen.

A low rumble escalated into another roar, harsh and grating, and the dragon lifted off again. The slow, heavy flapping of its wings hit her like drumbeats, discordant against the rhythm of her heart.

Its shadow crossed the tower again, but she did not move until the last throbbing beat faded into the distance. Then she seized her satchel, hitched its straps up her arms, and ran for the door.

Something black darted in front of her face.

She screamed, and he cawed at the same time.

"Divine's mercy, girl, I told you to stay put!" Aldram scolded as he backwinged and landed in the middle of the path. "I was gone what, all of five minutes? And you're trying to go gallivanting off on your own already, knowing that—that *monster* is out there? What chance in the world do you think you have?"

Adelinde blanched and sank to her knees. "I thought—"

"You certainly didn't," the crow snapped.

Her cheeks heated. "It was looking for something. You said you would feel its magic. I thought maybe if the dragon felt other magic, too, maybe it would be looking for its source. It could have been you, and—"

"The king's woods are west of the palace. The dragon was going south. Toward Ceresia, I'll have you know. It didn't feel me at all, and I was right under its nose." He flicked his beak toward the palace. "I've found something. I want you to come see it, see what you think."

Adelinde blinked. What was the chance he'd found it already? "Where?"

"Just follow me." He took wing and flew low, and she sprinted to keep pace.

He led her between ruined walls and over fallen columns, past clusters of flowers in overgrown gardens and into what must have once been the palace's courtyard. She looked over her shoulder twice, fearful the dragon might return, but it shrank away into the sky until it was no larger to her eyes than a sparrow might have been. It took a clean line south, she noted, and the fact gave her a chill.

It flew above the road.

"It's not far," Aldram said, hurrying her along. "Just around this corner."

Around the corner there was a flight of stairs. The crow disappeared into the shadows below, spaces light could not touch.

She faltered on the steps.

"Hurry!" His voice drifted back, soft as a breeze. "I want you to see this."

"I'm coming!" she called, exasperated. She dared not hurry, lest she fall. Having a limb broken or bent out of place would only serve to ruin everything. Unsurprisingly, the darkened cellar was still there when she reached the bottom of the staircase.

"Over here," Aldram said.

It took a moment for her eyes to adjust, but the room was not so dark that she could not make out the shadow of his black-feathered body against the far wall. Adelinde crept across the floor, avoiding rubble and loose stones. The nearer she came, the more clearly she saw in what little light filtered down from the stairs. Aldram sat atop a broken pillar, his head tilted toward the wall. No; toward a door. It was the same sort of stone as the walls and it bore no hinges, but it was set into a framed recess.

"Listen," the crow whispered.

Adelinde leaned closer and held her breath.

A soft, faint string of chirps and trills came from beyond the door.

"In there?" she asked in disbelief.

Aldram nodded.

There was no way to open the door that she could see. No knobs or levers, no latches or buttons. She searched the frame twice over before concluding it either required some sort of trick, or simply brute force. "Who could have sealed it inside?" It certainly sounded like the persistent song of a nightingale. Bastian had shown her one of the birds in the palace before, one of many creatures his father kept caged for entertainment.

But that one had been ordinary. This one sounded just the same. Surely an enchanted nightingale would sound different.

Adelinde slid her hands over the slab. "Are you certain it's magic?" Then she paused and leaned back with a frown. "How did you find this?" He'd scarcely been gone long enough to find another bird, let alone ask for directions or find out where the nightingale they were looking for may be. Why would he have started by looking underground?

The crow gave a raspy cluck and shook his head. "You'll have to trust me on this one, dove. I'm a bit more magical than you, what with the curse and all. What's in there... it calls to me."

As had the curse laid on Bastian. She drew back in alarm. "It's not the witch's magic, is it?"

"That, I couldn't say. Maybe. Maybe not. I'm not rightly sure. But it would make sense that she'd want back a creature she laid magic on, wouldn't it?" A hint of rue colored his voice.

She caught her lower lip between her teeth. He'd refused to go near the witch, following from a safe distance, stopping outside some invisible boundary outside her estate. Did Heldin want him back, too?

"There has to be some way to open it up. Most of the rest of the castle is in ruins, I don't know if there's any other way in." Aldram continued on, oblivious to the weight of her thoughts. He peered up at the slab and tilted his head. "There would have been, once. This is some sort of secret hatch, it seems, so there must be some sort of secret way to open it." He thrust himself from the pillar with a flap of his wings and fluttered to the top of the stone frame. It wasn't wide enough for him to perch, so he skimmed along it, wings beating frantically to keep him aloft.

Adelinde brought up both arms underneath him to scoop him out of the air. "I already looked there."

He squawked when she caught him, but grew still in her

arms. "No buttons, or hinges, or... or..." He hesitated. "No, it's going to be nearby, not right on the door. Blast me, if only I knew all of this place's secrets. Here, put me down. I'll look to the right, you check the walls over there." His beak bobbed to the left.

She lowered him to the uneven stone floor. "What am I supposed to be looking for?"

"Ever heard stories with a suspicious candlestick beside a secret door? Pull on it, and the door opens up. Try anything that protrudes." The crow hopped along the wall and pecked at any stones that jutted out just a little too far.

Most of what remained of the room was unadorned, but Adelinde still scouted each suspicious stone and shape. She pushed and pulled on anything that looked odd, though an embarrassed flush rose into her cheeks. "This seems foolish."

"Does it? I'd think it would be standard castle fare. You'll have to ask that prince of yours, once he gets back to himself." Aldram chuckled. "Why, I think it would be silly to build a castle and not fill it with secrets. You've got all that space, why not do something fun with it?"

She opened her mouth to protest, but as the heel of her palm came down on a jointed segment of a fluted false column, the stone sank into the wall. A gasp escaped her instead.

Aldram fluttered back a foot as something clanked and stone grated against itself. Slowly, the slab they'd found swung open. "Ah, you've done it!"

"I can't believe that happened." She stared into the shadowy gap. The nightingale's song trilled somewhere in the dark, never ceasing. The endless repetition made the hair on the back of her neck prickle.

"Well, what did I tell you? Castles and secrets. It's what they're made for. Come along." He hopped through the new doorway without hesitation, his sleek, glossy feathers disappearing in the dark.

"Go slowly," Adelinde called after him. "I can't see you." She made out a wall to one side and sought it with her fingertips. The stone was rough and unwelcoming, but at least it let her know where she was.

"Just follow the birdsong," he replied, closer than she expected.

She swallowed hard and inched forward until shadow took everything, and only the nightingale's voice remained to lead the way.

Ten

Darkness pressed against Adelinde's eyes until it hurt. She blinked hard to clear them, but it didn't help; there was no clearing the absence of light that squeezed the air from her lungs.

"That's it, girly, keep your feet moving," Aldram coaxed.

She followed his voice, though her heart thundered in her chest. The longer she kept her feet moving, the less likely she was to end up frozen in place.

The wall beneath her fingertips was textured, etched with carvings and reliefs she could not even imagine. Fear chased every image she tried to conjure right back out of her mind, leaving only the endless dark.

The dark and the birdsong.

The nightingale still sang, its long strings of chirrups and trills echoing off the stone.

"That's it," Aldram repeated. "Shuffle along, the floor's nice and smooth. There's a wall here, we're turning right. Are you still at the wall? Follow it around the corner. Keep going, dove."

"How much farther?" Her voice came out tight, strained, and it bounced off the walls the same way the nightingale's song did, distorting her sense of location.

"We're getting close. The magic's getting stronger. It shouldn't be too much farther."

Adelinde prayed he was right.

"Going left now," he prompted. "Put a hand out in front of you so you don't run into the wall."

She raised her other hand. Before long, she found the wall and turned to follow it. Whether they were in a maze or tracing the outer edge of a large room, she had no idea. "Now where?"

"Follow until the corner, then right."

How did he know? She didn't think he could see in the dark. "Aldram—"

"Trust me," he said. His voice was to the right; the corner came just after that.

When she rounded it, a soft hint of a glow greeted her eyes and her heart skipped a beat. Daylight? Or some sign someone had been down there? A dry, dusty odor greeted her nose, and she feared the latter was more likely. Daylight would have meant fresh air.

Aldram hopped along the floor and the dark outline of his body slowly separated itself from the floor as the glow brightened. "Just ahead. To the left. Almost there, now. Almost!" He picked up his pace, still bouncing instead of flying, and he disappeared into a new passage to the left, as he'd said.

The light was brighter there, though it was nowhere near daylight. Adelinde hurried toward it, all the same, and together, they spilled out into a wide room with stairs across from their hallway. To either side of the stairway, strange lights made of milk-colored glass cast the warm glow, illuminating all the treasures in the room.

Chests with gilded locks sat along the walls, their tops covered with bouquets of dried flowers and countless envelopes sealed with colorful wax.

Adelinde opened her mouth to ask where they were, but the nightingale restarted its song, its voice loud and clear. She spun toward the sound and her heart skipped a beat.

Atop one of the chests, surrounded by dried flowers, sat the nightingale.

It moved up and down as it sang, its wings of silver filigree tucked close to its sides. Its tail was spread to help it keep its balance on delicate wirework feet, and its beak did not move, though it trilled.

"How...?" She couldn't finish the question, unsure what she meant to ask. Step by step, she padded closer to the bird.

"Clockwork," Aldram said. "The enchantment is what keeps it moving. It'll sing forever, or until the gears wear themselves smooth."

"This is not what I expected," Adelinde admitted, though she still reached for it. It tingled when she touched it, like the gentle fizz of bubbles popping against her skin. Magic, she supposed, though a gentler sort than what she'd felt on Bastian when she picked him up. That kind had made her fingers smart.

"Nothing is what you expect when you deal with witches."

She lifted the bird and cradled it in both hands. It continued to sing, unbothered. "Was this what she meant, you think? Did she make it and leave it here?"

"She might have made it. I couldn't say who left it, though." Aldram's voice grew muffled and she turned to look.

The crow sat at the foot of what appeared to be another sealed doorway, pecking at the edges.

"Is that the way out?" Adelinde's eyes darted toward the stairway as she asked. That was the more obvious route out, but where did it lead? If there was another, easier opening into wherever they were, why had they gone in through the back?

And where *were* they? She looked again at the chests, the flowers, the letters, and an odd sense of discomfort crawled up the back of her neck and made her itch.

"Hmm?" He straightened and his feathers laid down so flat, it made him look long. "Oh, it's... Why don't you come over here and see if you can find a switch like the last one? I don't think I'd be strong enough to push it on my own."

"That's not an answer," Adelinde said.

"Oh. The way out? No, we'll have to go back the way we came." The bird paced back and forth in front of the slab. "But you promised you'd help me, that was part of our deal. Now I'm calling in that favor."

"This is about your curse?" Adelinde asked. She glanced at the doorway, but it was as plain and unadorned as the one they'd passed through before. "What's on the other side of that door?"

"The answer to my problems. Possibly. Probably." He fluttered his wings and hopped in place. "Just open it, girly. Leave the rest to me."

Adelinde moved the clockwork nightingale to one hand and joined him at the door. She saw no gaps or seams in the trim that might have hidden a latch, but the door did not look so firmly set, as if it had been open far more recently. Something about it struck her as strange and uncomfortable, but she looked for a way to open it, regardless of discomfort. She had promised to help him, and she wasn't going to go back on that now. She ran her empty hand along the carved stone, searching for whatever secret the door hid.

"That's it," the bird coached. "There's got to be some way to get it open. We have to get in there." He rocked on his feet, restless and agitated, nothing like the unshakable bird Adelinde had gotten to know. His eagerness left her uncomfortable.

"Did you know this was down here? Is that why you brought me?" That something needed to break Bastian's curse would be in the same place as what was needed for his struck her as too convenient to be coincidence.

"I didn't know. I'm lucky, that's all. That's all." But he bounced more insistently, and the more animated he grew, the more Adelinde wondered if that was the truth.

She leaned against the slab as she looked for a way to open it, and to her surprise, it shifted beneath her shoulder.

"Yes!" Aldram leaped and fluttered when it moved. "That's it, just a little more!"

Adelinde grimaced. Of all the people who could be tasked with moving a stone door, she had to be the worst. She put down the nightingale, braced her feet against the floor and heaved with all her might. The door groaned alongside the protests of her back and shoulder. She struggled to ignore them both and focused on the slow but steady movement.

The crow beside her gave a whoop of delight and scuttled in through the new gap.

Inch by inch, the slab scraped open and light spilled in to illuminate what was inside. Gold flashed in the warm light and gems glittered, begging for attention, but her eyes darted past those treasures to settle on one in particular—a jeweled diadem atop a bed of dried roses, all resting on the breast of a supine form.

Her pulse leaped, but the figure was cold and gray.

A statue.

Knowledge of where they were made her limbs grow cold and Adelinde stumbled backwards. The chests and dried flowers. All the letters left by admirers.

They were in Athanor's royal tomb.

A handful of jewels spilled across her path.

"Take what you want," Aldram said. "Not as if it's good for anything here now."

She gaped for a moment before she realized what had happened. "You're a thief." Betrayal flared white-hot in her chest and shame at how easily he'd deceived her colored her cheeks.

"Well, so are you," he replied flatly, casting a weighted look back at the clockwork nightingale that still sat on the floor.

Adelinde tensed and stared down at the enchanted trinket. It continued to sing, sounding for all the world like a living creature, bobbing up and down on its feet as its little gears worked.

"If you don't want anything, you're free to go on back,"

Aldram continued. "You've done your part and I can handle the rest from here. I'll be out to join you in two shakes of a tail feather."

"I'm not carrying stolen treasure for you," she spat back, but the crow disappeared into the shadows behind the door and said nothing else.

Indignant, she scooped the nightingale from the floor and made for the stairs. If there was any chance they led to daylight, they were a better path to take than the darkened, twisting hall they'd followed before.

Aldram said nothing to stop or dissuade her and she marched on in silence, fuming.

She should have guessed sooner that he was up to no good. He'd been sly from the beginning, wheedling for aid with a silver-edged tongue. No wonder he'd found the nightingale so swiftly; he must have known it was there from the beginning. For all she knew, he'd moved it there on purpose, knowing she'd be right beside the door he wanted open. She shook her head at her own naivety and stared at the steps under her feet.

The staircase turned sharp corners three times, but each twist brought new and brighter light, and at the first hint of fresh air, she sucked in a deep breath.

It was enough to soothe her until she reached the top step, rounded the corner into the ruins of the castle's lower level, and bumped into the dragon's black-scaled snout.

Eleven

Adelinde's scream was all but drowned out by the roar that tore free of the beast's maw. The crumbling castle above shuddered with the vibrations and a shower of grit cascaded from the ceiling.

The dragon lunged forward, but the gap was too small for its great head to fit, and Adelinde spun to flee as its teeth snapped shut at her heel. She bolted for the steps, but the dragon's head withdrew and one giant forefoot plunged in after her. It snagged her from the stairway and dragged her toward the hole in the wall through which one giant reptilian eye watched.

Adelinde struggled in the dragon's grasp, but it held her arms clamped tight to her sides. She screamed again.

A flurry of wings and claws exploded from the stairway and dove for the dragon's eye with an angry caw.

Startled, the dragon let go and Adelinde tumbled to the floor. She hit the stone hard and her leg twisted. The pop in her knee was followed by scorching heat and she collapsed, gasping in pain.

The dragon's forefoot withdrew from the tiny room, its former captive momentarily forgotten. She dragged herself toward the stairs.

Through it all, the clockwork nightingale sang.

"Can't leave you alone for a moment, can I?" Aldram snapped as he dove back in through a hole in the ceiling.

Adelinde stuffed the nightingale under her shirt and pushed herself to her hands and knees. Her injured leg objected and she humored it for the moment, keeping that leg out stiff while she crawled.

The crow darted after her. "There's no escaping that way, the wyrm will snag you at the door."

"Then I'll get out some other way," she said through clenched teeth. "I just need a minute."

Fear that the dragon would reach back into the stairway to try and catch her clawed at her heart, but she slid down the steps one at a time until she thought she might be safe. Then she straightened her leg out in front of her and sought her knee with both hands.

Aldram landed beside her. "You won't go anywhere like that."

"I'll be fine soon enough. I've dealt with worse." She set her jaw as she pushed her kneecap back where it belonged. Her fingers strained against her golden rings, but relief came with the pop. She sat straight and fumbled with her belt.

"Are you mad? There's a dragon out there! This is no time to be undressing!" The crow looked back, but while another agitated roar split the air, no claws came searching for them.

"Make yourself useful and find me a stick or something. I need to brace this." A good, tight cloth binding would be better, but she had nothing to spare for it, and she wasn't about to dig for cloth in the tombs below.

Aldram huffed, but he disappeared back up the stairs.

The moment he was gone, Adelinde resumed her descent. A weapon, on the other hand, would be useful. Surely there had to be something useful hidden among the gifts left behind for the dead.

"And I'll return it, as soon as all this is done," she muttered to herself. "Just like I'll return you." Her hand settled above the nightingale tucked close to her breast and she tried to comfort herself with the intent. No matter what Aldram said, she was no thief, but surely the dead would not begrudge her borrowing what she needed.

That, she told herself, was far different from picking up any of the gemstones he'd scattered across the floor.

It didn't take long to find a dagger among the gifts left for the dead, buried beneath decaying remnants of bouquets. She still held her belt with one hand and regretted that meant she couldn't tuck the blade beneath it, but her knee needed attention most. It wasn't the first time she'd dealt with such an injury, nor would it be the last, and knowing it would feel better after a few weeks of bracing brought a small comfort.

On the other hand, knowing she wouldn't be able to rest the injury any time soon brought none.

Something clattered down the stairs and she twisted in place, expecting to see the dragon's claws reaching around the corner the way a cat might fish in a mouse's hole. Instead, it was a stick.

Aldram was nowhere in sight, but she voiced a quiet thank-you just the same. The splint rings on her fingers chimed an anxious warning as she crisscrossed her belt around her knee to hold the stick tight against her leg. It wasn't a good brace, but she pulled it tight enough she doubted it would slide.

The chests lining the room offered useful handholds to lever herself upright. Adelinde's injured leg was a little unsteady, but the makeshift splint did help, and she tested her weight on that foot several times before she decided she would be able to stand. A low roar echoed upstairs and she grimaced. Running from the dragon was a different story, but she had no choice now.

"Back the way we came, then." She limped to the wall she'd followed into that chamber and rested a hand against it for support.

The dark still chilled her to the core, but what waited at the top of the stairs was worse. She gripped her borrowed dagger tight and shuffled along, sparing her injured knee from as much weight as she could. Running would likely make the injury worse, but she'd rather give herself a permanent limp than end up in a dragon's belly.

She pressed on.

"Where are you, girly?" Aldram's voice called from the chamber behind her.

She dared not reply, lest her voice betray her intentions. The nightingale kept on chirping, though, and she winced. How good was a dragon's hearing? Better than hers, she had to assume, given the dragon had managed to return without her hearing anything at all. The sound of its wings had been deafening before. How had it managed to sneak back to the castle?

The first corner came and she followed it with care. There was no way of knowing what might hide in the dark. Part of her wished she'd thought to see if the odd, milky-colored lights could be removed from the wall beside the stairs. The rest of her decided it was better if she did not know. If they were inside some hall of the royal family's tomb, the chance she was scuffling her way through a crypt was all too real.

"Keep going," she murmured to herself, even as a shudder rolled down her spine.

She wasn't made for this. She wasn't brave. She was just an herbalist's daughter who had never completed her training, who had dared to love a prince.

The soft glow of daylight appeared at the far end of what she prayed was just a tunnel, promising the secret doorway she'd opened before remained unblocked. Adelinde clenched her teeth and inched along with as much speed as she could muster without leaning too heavily on her leg.

No shadows darkened the room. No claws peeked over the edge of the crumbling ceiling. She hovered at the doorway for a moment, straining to listen for any indication the dragon might be hiding around the corner, but all she heard was a painful stillness behind the incessant song of the nightingale. *That* was a problem she hadn't figured out how to solve, and though she put a hand over it to press the fabric of her shirt close and try to mute its melody, it made no difference at all.

She'd just have to run. Run, and hope for the best. She'd have to make it back to the tower first, for she'd left her satchel of supplies there by mistake and she wouldn't get far without those.

Just run, she told herself. *Run for all you're worth and figure out the leg later.*

There were herbs among her supplies that would help with that, things that could speed her recovery and dull the pain at the same time. Yet even if she was able to reach them, the ruins of the old tower would do nothing to hold a dragon at bay. A single sweep of claws or tail would topple the thing on top of her, and then what?

Adelinde swallowed and turned the dagger in her hand, settling its cord-wrapped hilt more firmly against her palm. Such a tiny blade was unlikely to cause harm to such a great beast, but maybe it was enough to take it by surprise.

She sucked in a breath, counted to three, and bolted from the shadow.

A roar tore from the dragon the moment she stepped into the light, but Adelinde did not slow. Pain jolted up her splinted leg each time her foot hit the ground.

She clenched her jaw and struggled to gain speed against the strange, limping gait the brace on her knee gave her, but it wasn't enough. A massive shadow spilled over her and a clawed forefoot crashed into the earth to her side.

Adelinde squeaked, but kept running, the cold fear that shot through her system driving the pain out of her awareness and replacing it with panic. Her heart slammed against the inside of her ribcage as the dragon's other foot came down on her other side. Had it been any closer, she would have been crushed.

Is it playing with me? The possibility no more than brushed her mind before one of the beast's clawed forefeet swept toward her with the intent to grab.

She had nowhere to go and no speed to get her there, so she wrapped her free hand around the dagger's pommel and braced it against her stomach, blade outward.

The dragon's paw wrapped around her and the tiny dagger plunged between its scales and into the soft web of flesh between its digits. The monster yowled and jerked back, and Adelinde wasted no time in ducking beneath its claws to continue her flight.

That had been it, her one chance to catch the beast off guard and earn herself freedom.

Instead of pursuing her, the dragon drew back and reared up on its hind legs, a deep rushing of air the only warning of what was to come.

Adelinde cleared the last few yards and dove behind the tower's crumbling walls just as a torrent of fire struck the ground where she'd been and raked forward, howling like a gale.

She squeezed her eyes shut and burrowed farther backwards into the tower's shelter as the flames rushed past. Heat surged within the shadows as the dragon breathed flame across the landscape again. Sweat burst across Adelinde's brow and slid down her spine as the temperature rose. But the second burst of flame faded, and nothing more followed.

The long, slow scrape of movement warned her it was coming and she scrambled for the satchel she'd left behind earlier. Adelinde tore the nightingale from its hiding place within her shirt and stuffed it into the satchel, burying it in the middle of her supplies.

The dragon's shadow passed over the tower and she held her breath. She was small, but she still leaned forward with the satchel held close against her body, as if her fragile form could help muffle the enchanted bird's calls.

Heavy shadow crept farther and farther, until it blotted out the sunlight, and Adelinde prepared for the death she knew was coming.

Far behind the tower, a sharp racket of bird calls rose within the ruins of the palace and the dragon's attention was stolen away. It swept backwards and snarled in anger as its shadow withdrew.

Adelinde dared not breathe.

At last, the ripping snap of its wingbeats filled the air, and the last vestiges of darkness shrank away.

That held breath escaped her in a rush and Adelinde relaxed against the bulging bag in her arms. Sweat still trickled down her temples and she feared what things might look outside her crumbling shelter, but she waited for her courage to return before she dragged herself upright. The enchanted nightingale still sang away, but the notes of its song were more muted within the confines of her satchel, which she slung over her shoulder. Step by step, she inched to the door and peered out.

Smoke hung low and flames still flickered in what remained of the blackened grass. Adelinde almost touched the stone of the tower on her way out, but pulled back her hand at the last moment. Even without touching it, she felt the heat that radiated from it, and the moment she stepped into the sunlight, the breeze that washed over her brought cool relief. Her shelter had almost become an oven. Had any of the stones fallen to block the way out, she would have been doomed.

She dared a glance over her shoulder, to where the dragon was scaling the tower in pursuit of a tiny black speck that darted and lunged toward its face.

Aldram.

A knot tied itself in her throat, but she swallowed hard against it and forced herself to move.

He'd chosen to try and distract the monster, knowing what

risk that brought. She could do nothing to save him, and she would not waste the opportunity his distraction bought.

Adelinde stuck her borrowed dagger in with the rest of her things, gripped the straps of her satchel with both hands, and did her best to run.

Twelve

The ruins of Athanor gave way to unkempt forest. There, Adelinde finally slowed her pace. Her leg throbbed and the makeshift splint had rubbed her skin raw, but she'd escaped into the brush.

She sat at the first opportunity and adjusted the belt wrapped around her knee, wincing all the while. By the time her skin healed, her knee might be well enough to take off the brace.

After she'd caught her breath and her pulse slowed, she forced herself back to her feet and scouted out a branch to use as a crutch. It would make traveling easier, though it would force her to move slowly, and one glance at the time-worn road they'd taken to Athanor told her it was wiser to stay under the trees. She did not know if the dragon would pursue her, nor did she wish to find out. So she hobbled along, keeping the roadway in sight, until nightfall came and forced her to make camp.

There were still enough provisions in her bag to let her reach Ceresia's border, though with any sort of fortune at all, she'd be able to bolster her supplies with things foraged from the woodlands around her. She made no fire and ate in the dark, and after a time, she found the incessant song of the nightingale in her satchel grated on her nerves.

"Certainly the worst conversationalist of the birds I've traveled with," she muttered as she finished the fruit she'd rationed out for her meal. A pang of sadness mixed with worry hit her chest. Aldram had still been in the air when she'd made a run for the edge of the fallen city, but somehow she'd expected he would come after her.

Maybe that had never been his intention. She'd opened the door to the tomb he was after; maybe the help he'd offered to let her escape was all the repayment she could expect. With the door open, he'd had access to whatever treasure he desired and a good bit more. Maybe he'd gone back for it, after he'd seen she was safe. She could only hope he was safe somewhere, too.

As the night wore on, she gave up on the idea Aldram might rejoin her in the dark, and she let the nightingale's persistent melody lull her to sleep.

There were few splits in the road back to Ceresia, and what few there were, worn signs remained to point the way home. Adelinde rarely stepped foot from the shelter of the trees, though she made exceptions to examine the signposts.

The crutch made it easier to travel, but she could only walk for so long before she had to stop and rest. The days stretched on and still, she walked alone. All the while, the nightingale never stopped singing. By the time she was back within her home country, the noise had become little more than droning, easily ignored and forgotten. She only noticed it at night, when she rested her head against her satchel for a pillow and listened to it until her eyes grew heavy, and by morning it was nothing more than noise again.

She had traveled for close to a week before a rustle woke her in the predawn.

Adelinde jerked upright and grabbed her borrowed dagger

from the ground, but the crow poking at her satchel's closures squawked and leaped backwards.

Her mouth fell open. "Aldram?"

He huffed and dropped something beside his feet. "You get many other crows following you about, do you?"

She should have been relieved to see him. Instead, she was annoyed. "Where have you been?"

"Trying to find you. Mercy's sake, I never thought it would be so hard to catch up with a girl with a gimpy leg." He ducked to pick up whatever it was he'd put down, something red and glittering. He paused with it in his beak, as if trying to decide whether to resume his attempt to hide it in her belongings now that she was awake.

Adelinde's nose crinkled in disgust. "Did you steal that?"

Aldram tried to reply with the stone still in his mouth, then dropped it again with an agitated sigh. "Strictly speaking, no, I did not. Did you steal that?" He nodded toward the dagger that was still in her hand.

The very suggestion was enough to make her prickle. "No, I did not. I'm taking it back as soon as all of this is over." It would be a welcome distraction, she'd decided; the trip back to Athanor to return the dagger and nightingale would free her from having to watch the whole of her homeland celebrate Bastian's impending marriage to the witch's daughter.

"Then you can take this with you. You're just borrowing it for now." The crow plucked the stone from the grass one final time and stuffed it into Adelinde's satchel.

She didn't want it, but why she might carry a gemstone with the intention of giving it back instead of selling it, she had no idea. "What's it for?"

"Protection. Kings wear rubies to ward off evil, or so they say. I don't know that it'll do much, but it might help when..." He trailed off and for a moment, his dark eyes struck her as a little more human, filled with worry. "When you deal with that rotten old sorceress. I can't go in there to help you, but at least you'll go with me knowing I tried."

Her indignation softened, ever so slightly, and she reached for her bag's straps. "Do you know how much farther it is?"

"Oh, not far, now. You'll be there tomorrow morning, if not tonight." His eyes grew wistful as he spoke, then hardened again until they were merely the dark, glassy eyes of an ordinary corvid. "But I still expect your help when all this is over. A deal is a deal, and I'm still cursed."

"Maybe you should stay cursed, if it'll keep you from being a grave robber." She used her crutch to climb to her feet and turned to orient herself alongside the road.

Aldram fluttered to her shoulder. "As if you have any problem with treasure. You've got gold all over your fingers."

"My rings were a gift," she replied, with a little more heat than she intended. "It's different. And they're practical, besides."

"And you think a gemstone to protect you from evil isn't practical?" He sounded offended.

"Not when it's stolen. It works for kings because it's their rightful property."

The crow harrumphed. "Give it back, then, and I'll wear it myself."

"No. It's staying with me and I'm taking it back to Athanor after all this is over." She didn't know how she was supposed to return anything to the ruins of the castle, but maybe transporting them back to the fallen kingdom would be enough to clear her conscience. Surely there would be a proper place to leave them that didn't require her risking another encounter with the dragon.

"Ridiculous," he muttered.

Adelinde chose to ignore him and they walked for some time before he spoke again.

"Tell me about the rings," he said, more quiet than conversational, and not a question, either.

"What, these?" She raised a hand and tilted her fingers so the angled bands clinked.

"No, some other rings. Yes, those. I swear, you're difficult on purpose." His head lolled, giving the impression he rolled his eyes.

She rubbed a thumb against the underside of one of the rings. "I told you. They were a gift."

He hunched low beside her cheek. "A considerable gift for a peasant girl."

"But nothing to Bastian," she replied.

Aldram waited. His silence invited her to go on.

"I think that made it easier to take them, to be honest." Adelinde couldn't help but smile at the thought. It had been such a kind gesture, but had it come from anyone else, the precious metal would have forced her to refuse. "If they had been iron or bronze, they would have worked just as well and been every bit as valuable to me, but gold is plentiful to a prince. He said he didn't want anything that would tarnish or corrode, so he chose gold and had them made to fit me. He drew pictures of my hands. Marked which joints gave me the most problems and worked with the jeweler to design something that would keep me from hurting myself when they bent too far."

"A thoughtful gift," the crow said. "Sounds like a kind lad."

She smiled and paused to step over a fallen log. "He is. That's part of what made me love him. He's never tried to make me be anything I'm not. I don't have to be strong, or wealthy, or beautiful, or anything else a prince might want. He always loved me just as I am, and I would give anything to save him."

"Be careful making promises like that, dove," he said softly, and she took the notion he spoke from experience.

Adelinde examined his feathers from the corner of her eye. He'd already shared enough bits and pieces for her to see the similarities between them, though they'd sought to rescue the one they loved from different sorts of malady. "But she was worth it, right?"

"Worth everything and more," Aldram agreed.

She nodded. "Then it should be all right. Besides, she said she'd need three reagents to change him back, and we've already got two."

The crow ruffled his feathers. "That's why you've got to be careful now."

"I will be." Adelinde touched a finger to his head and stroked his feathers smooth. So far, she had evaded brigands and faced a dragon. How much worse could the final task be?

"It's late." The observation struck Adelinde as foolish as soon as it left her mouth. It had already been dark for several hours by the time they stood in the woods just north of Heldin's estate.

"And this is as far as I go," Aldram replied. He examined the trees overhead, looking for just the right place to roost.

She hesitated. "Maybe I should wait until morning." With as short as the witch's temper was, she couldn't help but fear what might happen if she roused the woman from slumber. If they were both cursed, would Bastian eventually be set free? Who would be left to save him? As far as Adelinde knew, there were only a handful of people who even knew what had become of him. She thought of Florina and stifled a snort.

"Sounds as if you already decided you won't. I'll be waiting here, then. Be careful." Aldram launched himself from her shoulder and spun a lazy spiral around her before he banked and disappeared into the trees.

Adelinde hated how fast he vanished, but she supposed they'd be back together before long.

She worked her way around the edge of the walled-in garden that surrounded the manor and forced herself to keep moving when she reached the front path. The windows were still illuminated, promising someone was awake and staving off some of her fear. There was no reason to fear Heldin tonight. For better or worse, they were on the same side —for now.

The door remained closed as she approached. Adelinde leaned the branch she'd used as a crutch against the wall to one side of the entryway. She didn't fear anyone thinking her weak, but she did not trust herself to navigate the witch's crowded workspace with the crutch propping her up. She thought she could walk without much of a limp now, though her leg would feel better with a few weeks of proper rest. Back home, she'd be able to sit while she worked.

And work she would. As soon as Bastian was free, she'd bury herself in whatever she could, ensuring she didn't have to hear about the wedding. She'd mix enough tinctures and dry herbal remedies to get her through the next season, and by then, maybe it would all be over.

She raised her hand to knock and the door creaked open before her knuckles landed.

This time, there was no one on the other side.

Heldin would be working in the back room again, Adelinde assumed. She adjusted her satchel and strode inside with her thumbs hooked under the straps. Muted as the nightingale's melody was, with the bird now wrapped and stuffed deep within her bag, its soft trilling struck her as noisy in the still of the witch's house.

She crept through the rooms, though she did not know why. They were bright, well-lit, and should have been inviting.

Then again, nothing about the witch was inviting.

When Adelinde reached the door to the woman's work room, she was not surprised to see an orderly arrangement of half-finished tinctures and tonics spread across the table, interspersed with bowls of crushed herbs and ingredients waiting their turn. The potion bottle she'd used to hold Bastian sat in the middle, still filled with soil, though a few colorful pieces of fruit peels rested on top.

Heldin stood beside a shelf, her back turned to the door, but the woman already knew she was there. Why else would the front door have opened itself?

"I see you've accomplished the second task without trouble," the witch said. "Or perhaps I should say I hear it." She tilted one ear in Adelinde's direction.

It was all Adelinde could do to keep from laughing, though she saw no humor in the situation at all. Without trouble? There was no doubt in her mind that Heldin had known the dragon would be there, ready to incinerate her and remove her from the situation without so much as a grave for flowers.

Instead, she mustered a polite smile. "It wasn't what I expected, but I believe this meets all the description of what you required." She slid her satchel from her back and let the bag rest on the floor, then sank to her good knee to retrieve the bird. She had bundled it with every scrap of spare clothing she'd packed, as well as the cloth that had been used to wrap bread and cheese and whatever other provisions she'd used up. With every layer of fabric she peeled away, the song grew louder, until the little clockwork bird perched on her palm and sang with all its might.

Heldin turned to examine the trinket with a speculative eye. "Yes," she concluded at last. "That will do."

"And I already know I can't help you with using this." Adelinde stood and carried the bird to the table. "So that's it, then? Just one reagent left, and then you can change him back?"

"Yes," the witch repeated slowly. Her attention drifted from the nightingale to Adelinde, a faint smile playing on her lips.

An uneasy chill traced the length of Adelinde's spine. "Well, what is it, then?" She didn't mean to sound demanding, but the way Heldin stared at her put all her nerves on edge.

"Why, dear girl..." Heldin chuckled, and the small, smug smile on her face twisted into a wicked grin. "The last reagent is you."

"What?" Adelinde couldn't seem to form the word as more than a whisper.

Again, the witch chuckled. She stalked across the room like a wildcat, her pace both smooth and predatory. "The most simple ingredient of all, though perhaps the most expensive, hmm? A wyrmstooth lily, its bloom to represent the opening of the curse. An enchanted nightingale, its song a cadence to guide the magic on its way. And a replacement, dear child. A vessel to hold the curse in the young prince's stead."

Adelinde felt as if her heart leaped and plummeted at the same time. She opened her mouth to speak, but no words came out, her silence only made more stark by the song of the mechanical bird she still held.

"What's the matter, girl? You haven't changed your mind already, have you?" Heldin taunted.

Her pulse soared. "No," she replied, though it took a moment to find her voice again. "That's all that's left? A vessel for the curse, and then Bastian will be free? He'll be himself again?"

"Of course, child. I am a woman of my word."

Adelinde didn't believe her for a moment. "I want to see him. I want..." *A chance to say goodbye* sprang to the tip of her tongue, but she gulped it back. "I want to see him whole and well before..."

The witch scoffed quietly and waved a hand. "You'll see him before the curse takes hold. It must leave him before it can claim you, after all."

"And then he'll be free, and I'll be... I'll be..." Her throat tightened and tears pricked her eyes. She couldn't make herself finish, but she didn't have to. They both already knew.

Her eyes darted to the bottle on the table and then her chest grew tight, too. Would she be bottled up and trapped the same way? Stuck in one place, left to suffer?

Would she suffer? She thought of the pain in her knee, the splint rings on her fingers, the aches and pains that had always come from joints that were simply too loose—and what it would be like to be trapped in a form that had none. Would it bring relief, or agony? Did it matter?

Would she even *know*?

Tears clung to her eyelashes and she squeezed her eyes closed, as if to hold more at bay. It didn't matter; she set that decision in the center of her mind and held it fast. The last thing she was certain she would know was that Bastian was free. And if she knew nothing else, perhaps that was a blessing of its own.

No one would tell her about the wedding festivities. She wouldn't hear the bells. She wouldn't hear the happy news of children in years to come, or how the witch became a hero by driving off the dragon before it could bring about Ceresia's end.

Bastian would be spared, but so would she.

"Fine." Her voice quavered with the single word. "I'll do it. I'll be your vessel, I'll take the curse."

A soft, melodious laugh burst from the witch. "Oh, dear child. Of course you will. You never had a choice." Her eyes glinted and she snapped a hand open.

The clockwork nightingale Adelinde clung to creaked to a halt in her hand, its gears seized as threads of light poured from its beak. She gasped and dropped it. The bird clattered to the floor and lay still and silent.

The strands of light twirled around the witch's fingers as she snatched Bastian's bottle and threw it to the floor.

"No!" Adelinde cried as it shattered. She scrambled around the table, toppling her satchel on the way, but it was too late. The bottle already lay in countless shards, the dirt scattered on the tiles.

To her relief, the lone, fragile earthworm twisted amid the dirt, unharmed by the fall or the glass. She scrambled sideways, around the table, to scoop him into her hands.

Before she could, the magic seized them both.

The threads of light the witch stole from the nightingale wrapped around her like vines and twisted tight, threatening to choke the air out of her. At the same time, they coiled around the worm—around Bastian—and made him writhe.

"Don't hurt him," Adelinde gasped, though she didn't know if she begged it of the magic or the witch.

Light sparked on his tiny form, glowing brighter as murky greens and smoky purples tainted the threads of magic that bound the two of them together, until the light consumed him and he began to change shape.

Her heart leaped into her throat as tears of relief flooded her eyes. "Bastian."

He reached for her, the light that enveloped him blinding but unable to hide the change. His hand found hers, his fingers warm and his grip strong. "Adelinde," Bastian rasped as he laced his fingers with hers and dragged her closer. "What have you done?"

She shook her head and leaned into him, let his arms wrap around her shoulders. Her voice failed her and her tears flowed free as the last of the curse's magic left his body and left him visible. Left him *whole*.

The curse swirled above them, dark and wicked, like a thunderhead turning the sky green before the hail.

Bastian hugged her until it hurt. "Adelinde—"

She pressed a finger to his lips before he could go on and smiled through her tears.

He took her by the shoulders. "Wait."

The threads of magic still tied around her grew heavy and cold and she gasped beneath the chill. Her whole body shuddered as the first wretched strains of the curse pierced her, body and soul.

"Wait!" Bastian begged.

Adelinde cradled his face in her chilled hand. "Please," she whispered. "Don't waste this."

Then the witch's magic collapsed inward, and her whole world went dark.

Thirteen

Bastian could do nothing but watch in horror as Adelinde shrank, her delicate frame folding in on itself until he was left with nothing but a tiny, twisting earthworm cradled in the palms of his cupped hands.

His breath caught and he shook his head, first with disbelief, then again with a feeling that was all but unfamiliar. His fingers curled in around the worm that had been Adelinde and his head snapped up so he could fix his gaze on the witch. His breath came quicker as the woman smirked at him, and rage filled every fiber of his being. It tightened in his chest and swelled until it grew white-hot, his pulse throbbing in his ears as he struggled to fill his lungs with enough air to speak. "What have you done to her?"

"Nothing at all," Heldin replied coolly. "It was her own doing. She took the curse willingly. To free you, dear prince, so that your wedding may proceed."

"Change her back!" The shout tore free of his throat and left him hoarse.

The witch rested a hand on her hip and looked down her nose. "And why should I do that? With you back to yourself, we all have what we want."

"You speak for yourself, witch," Bastian spat. "Change her back or I'll do it myself."

That yielded a laugh, one so light and tinkling that it grated on his nerves. "With what power?" Heldin asked. "Even your girl couldn't spare you on her own. Nothing will undo that curse but death."

"Then let it be yours!" He all but dumped the worm into one hand and swept his arm across the table, sending bowls and bottles crashing to the floor. From the wreckage, he seized a broken bottle's neck and leaped to his feet to wield it.

Wind kicked up, pressing against him, and the air seemed to suck out of the room as the witch loomed closer. She was taller than he recalled, magnified by magic, and her face grew dark as storm clouds. "How dare you? After all that's been done for you? Do not make me rescind this deal. There are other ways into power rather than—"

Shattering glass cut her short and her words broke with a gasp as a black mass hurtled through the window. Wings lashed around her head and claws tore at her face and a shriek rose in the witch's throat.

"Run, you idiot! Take her and run!" a man's voice shouted.

Bastian gaped for half a second, then curled his hand close around the fragile worm in his grasp and darted around the table. His boot hit something on the floor and he looked down in time to see a knife skid across the tiles. Without hesitation, he snatched it from the floor and ran. Behind him, the witch's screams rose louder, mingled with the angry cawing of a crow.

He didn't know where he was going. He raced through doorways and around corners until he skidded into a kitchen and almost ran into a scullery maid.

His heart skipped a beat when she spun to face him.

Not a scullery maid.

"Florina," he choked.

The bride his father had chosen for him looked from his face to the dagger in his hand.

He braced for her to scream or start another confrontation.

Instead, she hurried across the room. "This way," she said, casting a single, worried glance back the way he'd come. The noise had only grown louder.

Bastian stared in disbelief as she opened a door to the outside. She was helping him?

As if she'd read his thoughts, a timid smile cracked across her face. "Go."

He stared. "Why?"

"Because you're no use to anyone dead." Florina paused and a shadow of sadness darkened her eyes. "And I'd rather see you free."

For a moment, he didn't know what to say. Instead, he just nodded and sprinted for the door. He leaped a row of vegetables in the garden that greeted him, then vaulted over the low stone wall. The trees beyond promised shelter and he ran for it with all his might.

He had not gone far into the woods before a flurry of wings burst down through the canopy with a litany of low and angry caws.

Bastian stifled a shout as the bird descended toward him. He swung at it with the dagger, unable to see it clearly in the dark, unwilling to risk inaction.

The blade missed feathers by a hair and only made the bird angrier. It dove at his back with claws extended. "Move your legs, you cotton-crowned sluggard!"

Had he not just fled from a witch, Bastian would have screamed. He ducked away from the crow and ran until his feet faltered beneath him and he stopped, lest he fall. His shoulders rose and fell with each gasping breath he sucked in, and only when he felt steady enough to trust his grasp did he finally open his hand.

The tiny, fragile earthworm still twisted in his palm, leaving wet and sticky lines across his skin.

Ragged as it was, his breath caught in his chest and he held it there. The dagger was still in his other hand; he fumbled with it until he managed to wedge it under his belt. Vaguely, in the back of his mind, he became aware of the finery he still wore, remnants of the disastrous birthday ball he wished had never happened.

Slowly, he moved his now-free hand, one finger extended toward the worm's smooth body.

The crow dove past his shoulder.

Bastian snapped his hand shut and twisted to the side. "Stay away!"

The bird landed on the ground, none too gracefully. "A bloody fine thank-you that is! Adelinde—Divine's mercy, let me see!"

He twitched. How did the bird know her name? A talking bird, no less. Bastian's brows pinched together above his wrinkled nose.

Undeterred by his lack of response, the crow righted himself on his feet and hopped forward. "Adelinde!"

"Be quiet," Bastian snapped back. "You think I'm foolish enough to let you see her? You're a blasted bird!"

"A blasted bird who saved your hide, back there! Adelinde— She—oh, curse it all, what has she done? I told her to be careful, the moment I felt that magic swelling, I—"

"You spoke to her?" His heart leaped and his stomach turned at the same time. He'd only caught a fleeting glimpse of her tear-filled eyes before she'd been changed. "Was she all right? What was she doing? What did she say?"

"She was rescuing you!" The bird almost snarled. His wings fanned and his head bobbed in some strange gesture of agitation, a harsh reminder that he was an animal, whether or not he spoke.

Bastian drew back a step and his face grew guarded. "You spoke to her. You're speaking. You—"

"I'm cursed," the crow finished for him with an exaggerated skyward roll of his head. "What in the world are they teaching the young ones, these days? You'd think you, of all people, would know when you saw a curse. And Adelinde…"

Adelinde. Bastian's throat tightened and he opened his hand again, just to look at her. "Adelinde," he repeated. The sweetness of her name threatened to choke him.

The bird stared up at him, wings slumped. "She's… Oh, dove, why'd you trust her?"

The constriction in Bastian's throat only grew worse. She'd done it for him. "What am I supposed to do? Heldin said the only thing that'll undo it is death, I—"

Angry voices rose in the forest behind him. He grimaced and looked down at himself. He had to keep running, but he couldn't keep Adelinde in his hand forever. He'd crush her, or worse. If only he'd thought to grab a jar before he fled the witch's estate. He patted down the front of his coat before he recalled the coin purse in his pocket.

"Move! Move!" The crow's head bobbed as he snarled the words in a whisper.

Bastian dumped the coins into the pocket of his coat and dropped to his knees.

An unpleasant squawk escaped the strange bird. "What are you doing? You've got to run, she's after you!"

As gently as he could, Bastian tilted his hand to let the earthworm slide from his palm into the small leather purse. She tumbled instead. He grimaced, but didn't waste any time. His newly-freed fingers dug into the dirt.

"Not that, it's too hard. She's so soft. Get the good loamy stuff." The crow hopped closer to a tree and pecked at the ground to show what he meant.

Bastian abandoned what he'd grabbed and scraped a handful of soil from where the cursed bird sat. Why he was following the directions of a talking crow was a problem he'd have to work out later. He shoveled the gathered dirt into the purse with the earthworm and then pulled its strings tight.

"Now move!" The bird rasped. "Divine's mercy, how in the

bloody blazes are people supposed to look to you for leadership?"

"Oh, shut up, or maybe I'll try seeing if your death will undo this curse." Bastian climbed to his feet and sprinted on through the trees.

It didn't take long for wing beats to catch up. The crow glided along beside him as he ran, weaving between branches and trunks. "All you're doing is making me wonder what it is she saw in you. I can't imagine that sweet girl having any interest in such a rude-mouthed, mean-spirited boy."

Bastian clamped his jaw tight. He was not mean-spirited; he was running for his life, escaping from a sorceress who was supposed to be their ally, who had turned him into a worm. And if he was rude, it was only because the blasted bird had started it. But instead of trying to think of a retort, he kept quiet. Responding would only make things worse.

"You're welcome, by the way," the bird said. "Ungrateful brat. Do you have any idea how dangerous it was for me to dive in there and distract that witch? After everything I've done for your family, you can't even muster a proper thank-you."

"For my family?" Bastian scoffed. "I don't even know who you are."

"Aldram. And I wish I could say I had the same pleasure." The crow swooped across his path.

Why the bird was so cross with him, he had no idea. He considered asking, then thought of the witch he was attempting to leave behind and chose to save his breath. There would be time for questions once they'd escaped.

And when would that be? He didn't even know where he was going. Bastian exhaled hard and stared straight ahead as he ran.

He couldn't go back to the palace. He couldn't go anywhere the witch might think to find him. There was a dragon to the north and his father to the south, and it felt as if they closed on him like a vise. They could slip either way, east or west, to try and escape, but he hardly knew which.

"We need an alchemist. A mage, or something," he breathed to himself.

"Or a girl with a touch of magic in her blood?" Aldram asked dryly.

Bastian looked at him twice. "What?"

"She made you a love potion so you would forget about her and attend your assigned duties. A love potion. And you never stopped to doubt whether or not it would work, did you?"

"Adelinde's curatives always work." Not that a love potion was curative, although it might have helped his problems.

"Exactly! What other herbalist do you know whose remedies always work?"

Bastian slowed to a stop and the crow landed before him as he considered that. "She's good at what she does," he murmured lamely before he told himself it didn't matter. Whatever sort of gift or talent she might have, it couldn't help her while she was curled up in his coin purse beneath a clod of dirt.

He made his feet move and adjusted his direction. "We'll go west. Adelinde's family came from the west. Maybe someone there has more skills like her mother and can make a potion, or something."

"Or something," Aldram echoed sarcastically.

"What?" Bastian asked, annoyed. "You don't think it'll work?"

"You think I haven't tried every potion maker between here and the western sea? They're useless, boy! The witch already told you the terms of the curse." The crow hopped along beside him, with a flutter now and then to help him keep pace.

"Well, I don't believe her. She gave terms for my curse, too, and it's not how it was broken."

Aldram scoffed. "Because the curse wasn't broken, you dolt. All she did was move it from one victim to another!"

The prince stopped short. If the curse hadn't been broken,

did the original terms still apply? "Is there another way to break it, then?"

"Don't know. How was it meant to be broken in the first place?"

"I was supposed to beg for forgiveness. I don't know how, since I was stuck as a worm, but—"

Aldram shook his head. "No, no. That won't work for Adelinde. The witch's quarrel was with you, not her. An apology from her would do nothing."

"So that's really the solution, then." Bastian's shoulders slumped. "Someone is supposed to die." His hand hovered over the pocket of his coat where the coin purse rested, a prickle of fear coursing through his veins. It was obvious enough what the witch intended; the curse would persist until Adelinde's life was over.

Unless there was some other way to thwart the witch's power. Trying to kill her returned to his thoughts, but Bastian scrubbed his face with his hands as if to chase it away. Who was he to go against a sorceress? He'd already seen what her power could do, and there was little stopping her from changing him back into a worm.

He exhaled hard and stared to the west, then turned abruptly to resume his northward trek.

"I'm sorry, where are you going now?" Aldram followed him, and instead of being agitated, his voice now sounded wary.

Bastian fixed his eyes on the heavy shadow beneath the dark trees, where only occasional patches of moonlight broke through to illuminate the way. "I'm going to thwart the witch's hold over Ceresia, and once she has no more power over us, I'll figure out how to help Adelinde and have the whole kingdom behind me to do it."

The crow gave a quiet harrumph. "And how are you planning to do that?"

Determination set Bastian's jaw tight. "I'm going to kill the dragon."

Fourteen

"I'm sorry, *what?*" Aldram leaped into Bastian's path, his wings spread as if he could halt the prince's progress. He was still just a bird, though, and Bastian stepped over him as easily as if he were a log on the ground.

"I'm going to kill the dragon," Bastian repeated. Any other time, his own confidence would have surprised him, but he'd already made up his mind with such iron will that he doubted anything could dissuade him now. "Heldin demanded I marry her daughter, and in return, she would ensure the dragon left us alone. Well, killing the dragon takes care of that problem."

"Oh no, no, no." The crow shook his head and made a sweeping motion with his wingtips. It was strange, the way he moved them like they were hands, and the gesture made some strange familiarity prickle at the back of Bastian's mind.

He ignored it. "Oh yes. Taking care of the problem myself shows we don't need her. She can wield power against one of us, against me, but what is she supposed to do against an entire kingdom when they realize how she's tried to manipulate us?" It had always been manipulation, but this would be different, he was sure. The only reason anyone tolerated it was because they believed there was no other choice. After Erich's death, Ceresia's people had surrendered the idea any ordinary man could slay the beast. Erich had been a confident swordsman—far more confident than Bastian—but perhaps that had been his downfall. Perhaps he'd overestimated his own capabilities.

Aldram thrust himself off the ground with a few wingbeats and glided into a nearby tree. "Oh, brilliant. Kill the dragon with what, boy? With that pointy little dagger tucked under your belt?"

A fair challenge. Bastian glanced down at the blade with a frown. "I'll need a sword." And he couldn't very well go back to the palace to get one. Were there still any blacksmiths between the capital and the ruins of Athanor? He didn't know.

"You need some sense, is what you need," the crow retorted.

"If you don't like my plan, you're welcome to leave." Bastian suspected he would prefer if the bird vanished. At least then, he'd be able to do things without the endless onslaught of criticism.

A sharp bark of a laugh issued from somewhere overhead. "Not likely. Your sweetheart promised to help lift my curse when she was done with yours, and I'm holding you to it."

Bastian pointed at his chest. "Holding *me* to it? I didn't promise you anything!"

"Well someone has to make good on it, and since the two of you traded burdens, that makes it your job."

An oath leaped to the tip of his tongue, but Bastian swallowed it. "Fine." It was anything but fine. He would have preferred to pluck the bird and roast him on a spit. "But that means you've got to help me help you. First, the dragon, then whatever your problem is. That means I need a sword, and you're going to help me find one."

For a long time, there was no sound but the whisper of the breeze in the trees overhead and the soft crunch of twigs and debris beneath his feet.

Just when he'd decided the bird had abandoned him, a

reluctant response came. "There should be plenty of swords to choose from up in the ruins of Athanor," Aldram said. "You'll have your pick, and we've got to go that way to take care of... I don't think your girly could have done it, but you, maybe... well, it might work." His voice fell to something just shy of a whisper, as if he spoke to himself.

A curious itch stole up Bastian's spine, creeping between his shoulder blades. "What might work?"

"It's not the most practical means of curse-breaking, but if it works for your sweetheart, maybe it'll work for... It's this way, Your Highness. Tilt just slightly west, if you would."

The abrupt change in the bird's demeanor was enough to make Bastian shudder.

He adjusted his direction, all the same.

The crow had nothing else to say, though he drifted from tree to tree as if to guide the way. Daylight broke across the forest before Bastian found the will to break the silence.

"I don't know how to fight a dragon," he admitted.

"I assumed you didn't." The crow's response was light and breezy, hardly befitting the gravity of the situation they faced.

"Do you have any suggestions?" Bastian felt foolish for asking, but if the bird had been a person before, there was always a possibility.

Aldram considered the question for a long time before he replied. "They haven't got a lot of weak spots. You'll be better off with a big two-handed sword, so that you have a chance to stab deep. Slicing won't do anything against those scales."

One of his brother's disadvantages, Bastian decided. Erich had been skilled, but he fought with a one-handed short sword and a shield. If the dragon's hide warranted a greatsword, a short sword would have done nothing. "Where are its weak spots? Its eyes must be a vulnerability, right?"

"Yes, but if you're on the eyes end of a dragon, it's already too late for you to make it out alive. It's a wonder Adelinde was able to outrun the thing when it'd made up its mind to eat her."

Bastian almost tripped. "Adelinde faced the dragon?"

"To save you." The crow stopped on a low branch and turned one speculative eye his way. "Still trying to decide if that was the wisest choice."

She was so quiet, so determined to make herself small, that Bastian couldn't fathom her standing before a dragon's maw. His heart ached until his throat grew tight and he pressed a hand against his breastbone to soothe it. "She's braver than I could ever be, isn't she?"

"Likely, but maybe this is your chance to redeem yourself. There is a soft spot under a dragon's jaw, where its throat expands as it breathes fire. More like leather there than armored hide, and if you're under a dragon's mouth, it can't roast you. If it comes to that, get under her chin."

"Under the chin," Bastian repeated. "Got it. Where else?"

"Where its legs meet its body, that soft underside." Aldram fanned a wing to expose the downy black feathers underneath. "Its armpit, I suppose. Softer flesh to let it move freely. That spot under its front legs is where you need to be. With a long enough sword and a good enough strike, you might be able to hit its heart."

"Understood." So the next step would be finding a two-handed sword, then figuring out how he was supposed to reach. He had not seen the dragon himself, but Bastian had heard more than enough stories from his father's soldiers. It was a massive monster and even if he made it to the dragon's weak point, he wouldn't be any taller than its elbow. He'd need to catch it laying down, or else they'd need a trap.

That last thought rattled in his head for a moment before he did something useful with it. "What can you tell me about the state of Athanor's capital? That's where the dragon is, right? You must have gone there with Adelinde." What he wouldn't have given to ask her about that adventure. His hand skimmed against the pocket of his coat, almost a gentle caress.

Aldram heaved a much larger sigh than his stature

warranted. "It's all in shambles now. The castle is all but destroyed. The beast seems to like perching up on top of the ruins and they fall a little more with each takeoff and landing."

"Are there pathways up through the castle's remains? Did you see?" If he could climb to the monster's preferred roosting place and wait for it to land, perhaps he could get close enough to stab the dragon in its sleep. It was a long shot, but Bastian figured it was his best bet.

"Can't say that I did," the bird said. "Apologies. I was more interested in the tunnels underneath, since the old catacombs were what we used to escape."

Bastian brightened. "Catacombs? Can you tell me how to get into them?" Assuming they ran under the whole city, they provided the best route into the castle's ruins. If there was some entrance near the outer edges of Athanor's capital, he could slip in unnoticed, and surely the ruins of a castle would have a few swords laying about.

"Easy, lad. It sounds like you're hatching an idea, and I don't like it a bit." Aldram landed somewhere closer to eye level. "The dragon saw us go through the catacombs. I don't know if it's possible to get in that way again, and we've got to get close to the palace before we reach the back door. Right under it, in fact. There's little chance we'll make it without being seen."

"What if we go under cover of night?" Even dragons had to sleep.

"I don't know," the crow said. "Believe me, I wish I did. I don't even know if the dragon will be there when we arrive."

"Well, maybe we'll get lucky and it won't be home when we arrive. Can you get me to the entrance of the catacombs? Show me how to get through to the castle and climb up what's left?" It was the best plan Bastian could put together without seeing the ruins with his own eyes.

Aldram opened and closed his beak several times before he spoke. "I can get you to the old barracks, how's that? We start there. Get you properly armed. Then we worry about the dragon."

Bastian nodded in agreement. "It's a plan."

"Not a particularly solid one," the crow muttered.

This time, the criticism was fair.

Fifteen

"Is that a church?" Bastian asked several days later, as they stopped at the edge of the woods and peered out at the aging remnants of a structure in the clearing.

Aldram landed on his shoulder and tucked his wings close, but not before buffeting Bastian's ear. "What's left of one. Nothing but a hideout for brigands now."

"You've been here?" It wasn't exactly a surprise, given how many places a crow could fly, but Bastian hoped that meant they were on the right path. The bird had assured him several times that they were making good progress, but this felt more concrete. If Adelinde had passed by this same place on her travels with Aldram, he would feel better knowing it.

"With your sweetheart. Came to fetch those wyrmstooth lilies. Still don't know what the old hag meant to do with them." Black feathers ruffled, resembling the way the hair might rise along an irritated dog's neck.

Unconsciously, Bastian lifted a hand to smooth them back down. If Aldram minded being touched, he did not say.

No people came or went from the ruins, but there were recent signs of life. A wagon sat to one side of the structure, its bed still loaded with barrels and crates.

Bastian gave his head the slightest of tilts. "Brigands, you said?"

"Smugglers, most likely. Thieves spiriting things away from the ruins of southern Athanor." The crow flicked his beak toward the north. "We're right on the border now. Keep going that way and our path will intersect with the main road through Athanor. Take us straight to the capital, that will."

And the sooner they reached it, the sooner Bastian could look for help setting things right. He hadn't thought much about that; the part where he was supposed to slay a dragon still struck him as an insurmountable challenge. Yet there he was, marching off to try and do it.

He tilted his head again. "Brigands would have swords."

"Perfect for knocking that pretty blond head off your shoulders if you try to go down there. North, boy. We're going north." Aldram teetered on one foot to point with a clawed toe.

Bastian planted a finger on top of the bird's foot and pushed it back down to his shoulder. "Right after we check and see if these fine gentlemen can spare some supplies to make the trip easier."

"Given how we got into this mess, I should have assumed that you were terrible at following directions, yet you still manage to surprise me. You'd better hope they don't recognize you, Highness, or they'll tie you up and be after a king's ransom." The bird paused and gave him a sideways glance. "Or, a future king's ransom, anyway."

Bastian rolled his eyes and started toward the church. "Actually, I was planning on telling them exactly who I am."

"Adelinde's the one with all the sense in this relationship, isn't she?" Despite his complaint, Aldram stayed on his shoulder.

"She would probably agree with that." It was also possible she'd be right. Bastian had been afforded many luxuries in his life; an impulsive nature was one of them. Within the confines of

Ceresia's capital, his rank had always protected him from any negative ramifications that might have come with being so hasty to act. That had changed somewhat after Erich's death, but if anything, the protection made him bolder.

Bastian strode to the open front doorway and peered inside.

Half a dozen startled faces stared back.

"Good morning," he said.

All six brigands leaped to their feet, hands on their weapons.

Before they could draw, Bastian spread his hands before him at an angle that was half defensive, half placating. "Easy, easy. I don't want a fight. I want help."

One of the men barked a laugh. "Help? What help do you think you'll get here?"

Bastian pointed at the sword belted to the man's hip. "I need a sword. A big one, two-handed, as long as possible. Do you know where I can get one?"

"You don't look like you could lift it," the man replied.

"Fortunately, I'm stronger than I look. If the lot of you would be interested in helping me reach my destination, too, there would be a reward." Bastian skimmed the faces of the others, though none of them were impressed and several appeared to be sizing him up. Well, that was no surprise. He was a bit travel-worn, but he still wore the finest clothing money could buy.

But the men did not act, leaving the one who'd spoken first to do all the talking. The man drew his sword and thumbed its edge. "What reward would there be for your head, boy?"

Bastian shrugged. Somehow, he kept from making a face when the movement made Aldram's feathers tickle his ear. "Not as much as you'd get for helping me." He fished in his pocket for one of the coins he'd moved when he emptied his purse. When he withdrew his hand, the gold piece gleamed between his fingers. "I can buy the sword outright, though, if you'd rather let me go alone."

Six pairs of covetous eyes settled on the coin in his hand.

"Double that money," the leader said, "and we'll find you a sword."

Aldram huffed, but Bastian ignored him and reached for his pocket again. "Done."

The man returned his sword to its scabbard and strode to the doorway to take the coins. He clicked them together in his palm the moment Bastian deposited them in his hand. "Good. Right this way, ah, your lordship."

So they didn't recognize him. That was a small treat. Bastian followed him through the ruins of the church, past the smashed remnants of pews and into what had likely been a study or private prayer room. Now it was an armory, stacked with weapons, none of them in particularly fine condition.

"Take whatever sword you please and you can be on your way," the brigand said. He waited until Bastian stepped into the armory, then retreated into the ruined sanctuary.

Aldram leaned close. "They're going to rob you. You know that, right?"

"I assumed they would try," Bastian whispered back. All the same, he strode forward and reached for a blade to inspect. It was a longsword, but smaller still than what he suspected it would need to be.

"Look for one of those great big claymores the warriors from the south carry," Aldram said.

"It'll be enough of a miracle if I can wield a regular two-handed sword. Let's not push it." Another sword caught Bastian's eye and he freed it from a jumble of weapons standing in a barrel in the corner. Its blade sported dirt and rust spots, but it was almost as long as he was tall. "This should do."

The crow turned his head to peer into the sanctuary. "Hope you're ready to fight with it the moment you step through that door."

Bastian rolled his eyes, but a hole in the ceiling caught his attention. Would it be worth it to climb out and just avoid dealing with the brigands again?

"If you're hatching another scheme, leave me out of this one," Aldram whispered.

"I thought birds were made for hatching," Bastian whispered back.

The crow scoffed, but before he could offer a retort, a shadow darkened the doorway.

The leader of the brigands loomed there, the corners of his mouth downturned. "If you're asking for help, I didn't catch it."

"Just asking if you had a whetstone. I think this one will do, but it needs to be cleaned, sharpened, and oiled before I set off." Bastian gripped the hilt with both hands and gave the blade an experimental swish. It was long enough it almost reached the other walls, and the brigand took a step back out of reflex.

"Of course, your lordship. Of course." The man motioned with both hands for Bastian to step from the armory.

He did, but he kept both hands on the hilt of his longsword. As he expected, the rest of the men were standing, waiting for him with their weapons drawn.

"Before we get to that, though," the leader said, "we couldn't help but notice we only asked for two coins, and there are six of us here right now."

"To be fair, you were the one who promised me a sword for two gold coins." Bastian's nerves itched, but he forced himself to remain relaxed, even as the crow on his shoulder tensed and hunched close. "It's hardly fair for you to change the agreement now."

"Oh, no change at all. It's just that whetstone and oil, you see," the brigand drawled. "They're in shorter supply than rusty old weapons. Four gold for the tools, your lordship. That sounds fair to us."

Bastian shifted the sword to one hand and leaned it back against his shoulder. "Or..." He raised a finger.

The ruffians shifted, expectant and uneasy.

"You could pack those supplies and some others, food and

the like, and escort me to the capital of Athanor." He offered his best and most winning smile.

The men just blinked.

"Athanor's in ruins, boy," someone said. Not the leader, but a harsher, more gruff and surly voice.

"And guarded by a dragon," Bastian added. "Which is why I'm headed that way. I mean to slay the dragon. Come with me, aid me in getting through the city to the dragon's roost, and we'll split the treasure in its hoard."

Aldram gave a startled squawk. "I beg your pardon? You can't just go around giving away other people's stolen treasure!"

An angry roar burst from the men.

"It's the bird!" one shouted.

"That crow from before!" said another.

Bastian glanced at Aldram from the corner of his eye. "Oh, you've met, have you?"

The crow hunched forward and fanned his wings. "And there were a lot more of them then. Take your sword and go, boy, before the rest of them come back."

Before Bastian could move, the men shuffled backwards to block the door. The leader posted himself in the front. "Give us the bird."

"Why? What did he do?"

"I, ah..." Aldram cleared his throat. "I may have done something with a bag full of gems they'd left on top of a barrel."

Bastian's head snapped around. "You're a thief?"

"Hey, you're the one promising shares of a dragon's hoard to these louts. That hoard is the amassed wealth of all Athanor, gathered into one place, and it rightfully belongs to Athanor's crown." The bird nodded as final emphasis.

"Well, the king of Athanor's dead," one of the brigands said.

"Which means it's ripe for the picking," Bastian concluded.

Aldram scoffed and flapped. "If anyone deserves that hoard of gold, it's me. You wouldn't even know it existed if not for me."

Bastian reached up to smooth the feathers down the bird's back and received a sharp peck on the hand. He jerked it back and considered being offended, then decided he'd brought it upon himself. "Then you can have a cut, too."

"What would a crow want with a dragon's hoard?" one man whispered.

The fellow next to him cupped a hand beside his mouth to whisper back, though he was near enough it did nothing to mask his words. "Crows do like shiny things."

"Speaking of," the brigand leader said, "what sort of cut are we talking, here?"

Until that moment, Bastian hadn't realized the men were even considering his offer. "Well, ah... Since the bird did find it, and I'll be doing the dragon slaying, I say we should get the larger cut. We'll split it three ways. A third for me, a third for the crow, and a third for the lot of you." The man looked like he was going to protest, so he raised a hand to stall any complaints and went on. "That seems more than reasonable, and in fact quite generous of me, considering I'm not even asking you to fight the dragon. Yours is the safest job of all, since the bird is going to be assisting me by distracting the beast so I can kill it."

"I am?" Aldram wheezed.

Bastian continued as if the bird hadn't spoken. "Just provide supplies for the trip and fixing up my sword, help me find a way up to the dragon's lair, and I'll handle the rest. There are bound to be more treasures scattered throughout the ruins of the city, besides. You'll be free to gather whatever you please while I take care of the slaying."

A few of the men exchanged thoughtful looks.

"It is an easy job," one murmured to another.

"Old Blackscales will be distracted, meaning the city'll be safe to roam."

"Even ten minutes to raid old Athanor would make us richer than ever."

"All right," the leader announced. He stepped forward with his hand extended. "Listen, mister... ah..."

"Bastian." He clasped the brigand's hand for a firm handshake.

"Harrald," the man replied. "And you've got yourself a deal."

Sixteen

For all that Harrald's crew was a handful of robbers, they proved to be decent companions, rough edges and all. They'd packed a good assortment of foodstuffs for the trip and shared generously whenever they made camp each night. They feared nothing in the woods and they knew the way well, and between their experience and Aldram's directions, travel was easy.

Any time they stopped, they took turns helping Bastian grow comfortable with the longsword in his hands, and day by day, he grew more confident with the blade—and more determined to see the task through.

He rested easily when Harrald built a campfire that night, for he found comfort in the ground they covered. Not because it put time and distance between him and his problems, but because the ease with which the northern region could be traversed brought relief for what he'd feared Adelinde had endured. She'd made this same trip for his sake, and walking such distance would not have come easily. Her legs did not bother her in the same way her hands did, but any time they'd gone on expeditions in the forest together that lasted more than a few hours, her knees and hips brought her pain—sometimes for days afterward.

Did she hurt now? He slid his palm over his pocket, her presence there reassuring and yet far from comforting. His fingers dipped into his pocket and he pulled the coin purse free. It was soothingly warm, even with the campfire beside him, and he stroked the suede as he wondered how she fared. It was hard to tell if an earthworm was happy. He'd added a small scrap of fruit to the soil inside earlier in the day, worried about whether or not she was hungry, but he truthfully did not know how one was supposed to care for a worm.

"I'll fix this," he murmured as he held Adelinde's purse between his palms, not for the first time and likely not for the last.

On the other side of the campfire, Harrald cleared his throat. "You must be in a sorry way, making promises like that. Though I suppose it would take a hefty debt to make a man face down a dragon for its hoard, eh?"

Bastian blinked twice before he understood what the man meant. To the eyes of the highwaymen, he was a nobleman in dirty finery, sitting beside the fire and whispering reassurances to a coin purse.

Heat rushed up his neck and he was grateful for the firelight and the way it would hide his flush. "Oh, no, it—that's not—"

"There's no shame in falling on hard times," the leader of the brigands replied, and for the first time, his weathered face softened. "It happens to all of us, lad. But if you knock old Blackscales off his tower, you'll be changing a lot of people's fortunes."

It was hard to imagine any of the men escorting him cared about the fortunes of others, but the men nearby all nodded.

Bastian supposed it was true. He meant to strike down the dragon for Adelinde's sake, but it would help Ceresia, too, and all of his country's people. It would help Athanor, though the kingdom was all but abandoned. At least if the dragon died, those who had fled could return home and rebuild.

Still, Adelinde was his reason for acting, and it did not sit well with him to pretend it was anything else.

"It's not like that," he managed at last, though his face was still hot as the flames in the fire pit. "It's—I have a curse to break."

Harrald's brows shot upward and he and two of his companions turned to look at Aldram.

The bird froze in the middle of preening his wing.

"Not him," Bastian added.

"Well, excuse me," Aldram put in.

Bastian shot him a glare. The bird had been kinder for the last several days, but the edge to his corvine tongue remained. Ignoring it grew more difficult, but he kept himself from responding to the bird. "It's my... my intended. Adelinde."

All three of the brigands turned back his way, their bewilderment clear. A moment of silence dragged past before one spoke. "She's a purse?"

"*Inside* the purse," Bastian said, exasperated.

The men only grew more troubled. "She's shrunk down?"

"Worse." Aldram either ruffled his feathers or shuddered, it was hard to tell which. "She's a worm."

For a moment, the brigands were silent. Then, uproarious laughter burst from all three gathered around the campfire.

"You're off to kill a wyrm to save a worm?" Harrald wiped the corner of his eye with his thumb, but did not stop laughing.

Bastian did not appreciate the humor. "Whatever it takes, I'll do."

"Just dump her out in a garden, boy." The brigand leader waved a hand. "Safer and easier and there are a thousand girls out there who would pine for a lad like you. You can raid the edges of Athanor with us, go back home wealthy, and choose at least a dozen who tickle your fancy."

"I don't want a dozen," Bastian snapped back. "I want

Adelinde. She's the one who's been there for me. Who sacrificed everything for me. I can't just turn away from her. She needs me. She loves me."

"She's a worm."

"I don't care!" This time, the heat that stole up his neck was anger instead of embarrassment. "By any shape or any name, I'll always love her. Just the same."

"Poetic," Aldram muttered sarcastically.

Bastian glared with such heat, even the crow shrank. He thrust himself from the ground and slid the coin purse back into the pocket of his coat. "You're all welcome to think me a fool, but I'm not changing my mind. I will reach Athanor, slay the dragon, defy the witch, and find a way to set Adelinde free."

"All right, all right. Simmer down, lad." Harrald patted the air as he spoke, but the outburst had already drawn the attention of the other men, who had been standing watch and gathering firewood to get them through the night. They stood about, watching as their leader tried to smooth things over. "I don't mean anything by it. If you love her, that's grand. Worm and all. Just be sure she's worth the sacrifice, lad, because what you're heading out on is a fool's errand."

"I know that." Bastian's shoulders bunched, but he made himself breathe deep and exhale hard. Some of his frustration leaked out with that breath. "I know. I just—it's my fault, and if I'd just listened to her, maybe this wouldn't have—"

"Worrying about would-haves doesn't help in situations like this." The brigand leader leaned over and pulled something from his bag. A bottle, it looked like, or a flask. He stood with it in hand, circled the fire, and unfastened the stopper before he proffered the drink. The moment Bastian took it, his free hand landed on the prince's shoulder and pressed down until Bastian sank to sitting. "Just rest for now, lad."

Bastian stared at the dark glass bottle in his grasp for a moment before he raised it and took an experimental swig. The liquid that rushed down his throat was hot and bitter. He coughed, and Harrald thumped his back.

There were fewer things he'd tasted in his life that were less pleasant. He returned the bottle and wiped his mouth with the back of his hand. "How much longer until we reach Athanor's capital, anyway?"

Aldram made a sound that could only be described as a frown. "We're already here." The crow shrugged before he moved to a new tree.

Bastian glanced around the forest with doubt. It had been a long time since he'd visited Athanor, but he didn't recall there being a forest so close to the city.

"The bird's right," one of the brigands said. "Past that patch of brambles there, the city waits, but it's too dark for us to see what we're doing. If Blackscales is there now, none of us saw him, but we're far enough into the woods that the fire shouldn't show. We'll cross into the ruins first thing in the morning, and once we find your path, you're on your own."

"Until we can divvy up that hoard," Bastian concluded glumly. He was the one who had chosen this task, but it would have been nice to have assistance.

"Until then," Harrald agreed as he took his own drink from the bottle. "But for now, all we can do is rest up. Settle your nerves, lad. You're almost through."

Almost unconsciously, Bastian let his hand return to his coat pocket, where Adelinde's purse lay close against his stomach.

He could only hope that was true.

Seventeen

The weedy brambles and saplings always made the thickest scrub near the edge of the forest, where they could stretch away from the shade of mature trees and steal sunlight for themselves. Bastian's eyes traveled across the grassy remains of what had once been a great city and then climbed the pale stone of the castle.

For the first time, he quailed.

He should have known.

"Oh no," Aldram almost groaned.

The dragon perched atop the highest peak of a crumbling tower, its tail swishing like that of an agitated house cat.

Bastian watched its languid movements with a cold knot of dread winding itself tight in the pit of his stomach. "It's bigger than I thought." And it was there. Its head turned their direction, as if looking for something, and he shrank back into the underbrush out of instinct.

"Not looking good, lad," one of the brigands said. Five of them hung back, sheltered by the thick and thorny brambles, though Harrald had stepped forward to survey the landscape. He said nothing, but his frown said enough.

Bastian made himself swallow. "Once I figure out how to get

into the ruins of the palace, the dragon will be distracted. The rest of you should be able to gather up whatever loot you want while I..." He trailed off and gave his longsword a gentle swish. It had grown annoying to carry, day in and day out, but there hadn't been a scabbard for it and there were few other options. It would serve its job soon enough.

One way or another.

"I thought the agreement was we should help you find a way into the castle?" Harrald scratched his chin as he stared up at the beast. For all that the dragon was searching for something, the man remained calm.

"Oh, you care about the agreement, do you?" Aldram had taken to riding on Bastian's shoulder most of the time, and he stretched himself out tall to peer over the top of the prince's head.

Harrald sneered back. "I may be a robber and a thief, but I'm a man of my word. Wait here a bit, your lordship, let us have a look around. Maybe we'll find a way in before you run out there and get yourself roasted."

Bastian had not taken the time to consider how he would handle the dragon's fiery breath, and the thought of it now made him blanch.

"Fair enough," Aldram said. "Into the brush, Bastian. Let them have a look. Maybe we can think up a strategy of our own while they search about."

Without a word, Bastian backed through the narrow path that led through the brush. Harrald retreated too, and the brigands split into two groups. They headed off, three men venturing east and three west, and that left Bastian to sit on the narrow game trail and stare at the palace, perfectly framed in the tiny gap in the trees.

The dragon's head swung back and forth, its eyes glinting in the sunlight as it searched the southern reaches of the ruins and their meadow.

"It keeps looking this way," Bastian murmured.

"Watching for us," the crow lamented.

"What?" Bastian tore his eyes from the beast to look at his companion.

"The dragon knows we're here. Knew I'd come back. Blast it all, I knew going into that mansion was a mistake, but Adelinde —" Aldram exhaled hard and his head drooped. "Divine have mercy on us. I'm sorry, Your Highness. This is my fault."

"I'm sorry," Bastian faltered. "I don't understand how."

Aldram shook his head as if scolding himself. "You might have made it into the castle to do the killing on your own, but I was there. I broke that window, trying to help, and now she knows I'm alive. Where else would I go? The root of my curse is here. I had to come back, and she knows."

The witch. He should have guessed sooner. It wasn't the witch's power that could keep the dragon at bay; it was the witch's power that kept it *there*. That was why she could drive it off. Why she could make such a promise to his father. Why his brother had died. Bastian's jaw tightened and he squeezed his eyes shut.

He didn't know if the crow's presence was what had given away what their next action would be, but he couldn't prove that wasn't it, either. That the dragon might see them before they reached the castle had always been a possibility. All he could do now was brace himself and move forward.

"It doesn't matter," he said at last. He still had to wait for the others to return from scouting, so he took his longsword and some of the supplies from the bag he'd been given and chose to make the most of his time. The blade would be as sharp as possible before he reached the dragon's tower. It would cut through leathery flesh with ease and kill with one strike.

One strike was likely all he would get.

"Don't know how you can say that," Aldram muttered, but he didn't argue anymore. It was clear he'd chosen to feel sorry for himself, and nothing Bastian said would change that now.

For a while, Bastian scrubbed at the blade with the sand and vinegar he'd been given to clear away the rust. The blade was clean, but the hilt was not, and he did not want loose grit or flakes hindering his grip. His eyes stayed fixed on the dragon and the pale stone of the palace beneath its hindquarters.

"I came here sometimes, when I was young, you know." He wasn't sure why he said it; Aldram hardly seemed like he wanted conversation, but the crow turned one dark eye his way and Bastian went on. "King Dalmar was my godfather. My father says they remained close friends until the dragon struck and he... he died." The words put an odd knot in his throat. He hadn't thought of such things in so long, he hadn't expected it would still bring such emotion.

Aldram studied him until the silence grew heavy. Then he finally turned toward the city, himself. "What was he like, in your eyes? The king? Was he a coward, like the stories say?"

Bastian snorted a laugh. "Far from it. He was one of the bravest men I ever met. He would have given anything for his people. In the end, I suppose he did." He paused mid-stroke with his rag. "But he could be hard. Abrasive. He was gentle to his wife, my aunt Emilia, but he was tough on me. Wanted me to be stronger than I was. Always thought I could be more. He pushed so hard and never seemed to have any patience when I fell short of his expectations."

"I'll bet you hated him for it."

"Not at all." Bastian cracked a smile. "He'd always say, 'Baby birds don't learn to fly without a push, Bastian, and neither will you.' But that made me braver, I think. He would have thrown me from that dragon's roost if I'd had wings, and called me an idiot if I didn't make a good landing. But he would have had me soaring in no time. I'm sure of that."

"Hmm," was all the more response Aldram gave.

They sat together in silence while Bastian scrubbed, the gritty rasp of the rag against the steel a harsh rhythm of its own beneath the cheerful birdsong in the woods.

Eventually, his hands tired, and he looked down at his work

as he wiped away what remained of the sand. "Huh. Look at this." He tilted the hilt and ran his thumb over an etching in the cross guard, previously hidden by rust and dirt. The sculpted petals of the lily did not yet shine, but they stood out.

Aldram straightened. "Wyrmstooth. From the Ceresian army?"

Bastian shook his head and wiped his hands clean. "We don't use that emblem on the swords anymore. I wonder how old this is."

"Wyrmstooth," the crow murmured to himself as his attention drifted back to the dragon. "No. Wyrmsbane."

"Wyrmsbane?" Bastian repeated.

"Every legendary sword needs a name, doesn't it? And this, boy..." Aldram chuckled. "This is the stuff legends are made from. Look there, your friends are back. Let's hope they have good news." He leaped to the prince's shoulder and made himself comfortable before Harrald and his companions reached them.

Bastian rose to greet the brigands.

Harrald spoke first. "Well, we've got news. Not sure if it's what you want to hear, but it's news."

"It can't get much worse than the part where there's a dragon over there, waiting to roast me." It was only half jest, and Bastian saw it was taken as such in the deepening of the fine lines at the corners of Harrald's eyes.

The man spoke anyway. "Well, there's not much to see on our side of the city. Signs of someone having been here, footprints in mud and ash and the like, but it doesn't look as if whoever it was survived. Big swath of land blackened from dragon fire. We followed the trail, because it looked like it came from the palace, but the dragon turned our way and there was no way to go any farther without being seen."

Which meant any passages in that direction would not help.

"That must have been where Adelinde and I were. The rotten lizard almost got us, and it was on that side of the city." Aldram flicked his beak toward the east. "There's a passage into the royal tombs under the palace there."

"Royal tombs? Is there any way they might be connected to a church somewhere in the city, or tied to catacombs under a graveyard?" Bastian tried not to sound too hopeful.

"We didn't see any church or any sign of gravestones," Harrald said.

The crow gave a thoughtful hum. "They'd be on the west side of the city. There was a grand church there. I don't know of any connections to the royal tombs, but maybe..."

Bastian knelt to put his supplies away. He'd leave the bag there, in the care of Harrald's crew, though he did not believe he would get it back. Fair enough, he decided. It hadn't been his to begin with. "The others should be getting back soon. Maybe they'll have found something better."

They waited another half hour before the other group returned.

"Good news for us?" Harrald asked.

The three men shook their heads glumly. One opened his hand to display a collection of coins. "Plenty of things left around the ruins for us, but nothing for the boy. The best we could find is a handful of buildings with roofing. Might be able to sneak from one to another."

"Doesn't sound promising," Aldram said.

Bastian scooped up his bag and extended it to the nearest man. "We'll just have to hope for the best. Hold on to this for me. No sense in wasting time."

Harrald scratched the back of his neck. "Shouldn't you at least wait for nighttime? Go under the cover of night?"

"Dragons see just as well in nighttime as day." Aldram shifted from one foot to the other. "Actually, we may stand a better chance going in from the west. It's getting toward afternoon and even a dragon can't look into the sun."

"West it is." Bastian adjusted his grip on his longsword and wished he had a scabbard for it. "While the dragon's distracted, the rest of you feel free to take whatever you can find from the ruins. Just remember, no touching the hoard until the two of us are there."

"You've got our word," Harrald said, the rest of the brigands behind him nodding along in confirmation.

"For whatever it's worth," Aldram muttered.

Bastian raised a hand to hush him and started toward the west end of the city. The sun was halfway between the sky and the horizon, and even from the dragon's vantage point, it would be hard for the beast to look his way without the interference of the sun's glare. "I'll need you to figure out the best path through the city," he told the bird on his shoulder.

The crow scoffed. "The best path is underground, but there's no other way into it."

"Then find me the second best path. Don't be difficult."

"You're the one marching off into a dragon's lair." Despite his complaints, Aldram flitted ahead and then darted out between the trees.

Bastian could only hope it was to devise a way through the ruins, and not to abandon him at the edge of the forest, leaving him to fight alone. He continued until he found what he thought was a good exit through the brush, then stopped to wait for the crow. His hand drifted over his pocket. "Wish me luck, Adelinde."

From what he could tell, she did not, but he chose to imagine she had anyway.

Just when he'd decided to try and slip from the forest, Aldram burst back in through the canopy overhead and nearly scared him out of his wits. The crow landed on a spindly branch and the way his head remained still as the rest of him bobbed and swayed with his perch was mesmerizing.

"Well, I hate to say it, but your friends seem to be right." He pointed with his wing feathers. "Straight out of this neck of woods, there's an old house that still has half its roof. The others are spaced out a bit, but you should be able to zigzag between them."

"And here you didn't want to have them along." Bastian crept to the opening of the forest to see what he meant. The dragon still looked toward the south.

"I still think you're nuttier than a squirrel in spring for trusting them, but I can admit when someone else has good advice. The hardest place will be the gap between the guard house and the front of the palace. I'd tell you to take a side door, but I don't know if they're barricaded. The front doors have fallen in, so they're the surest way into the palace." Though the dragon was still far away, Aldram kept his voice down.

Bastian did, too, unconsciously mimicking the bird. "Front it is. Are you ready?"

"Not in the slightest, but you already know that and I don't know why you're asking me."

"Good. Let's go." He angled his sword to reduce the risk of it glinting in the light and took off at a run.

He darted from the forest to the ruined house before the dragon's head swung their way. The roof certainly did not cover half the building. It was scarcely more than a corner, and the timbers were scorched and blackened from dragon fire.

"Be still," Aldram whispered. He leaped to the edge of the wooden roof and hunkered down low, his dark feathers blending in with the burned wood.

Bastian dared not try and look on his own. He focused on keeping his breath even and eventually, the bird dropped back to his shoulder.

"Go. North. Quickly."

To the north, the building that offered shelter had no roof, but part of the floor of the second story remained. Again, Bastian ducked into it to hide while the crow watched for the dragon's attention to move elsewhere.

The flow between buildings was smooth, seamless, though the closer they got to the palace, the more Bastian found himself wishing he had some sort of armor. It wouldn't protect him from the dragon's flames, but it might have helped against falling debris, and he couldn't imagine he'd make it up the castle's tower and all the way back down without the beast knocking something loose.

"Last one," Aldram whispered as they came to a halt within the guard house. The rest of the castle's wall had fallen, so it was clear to either side, but the expanse of what had once been the castle's yard stretched on at least three times the length of what he'd run between the other buildings.

"Tell me when," Bastian whispered back. He gripped the sword in both hands now, though he didn't know what good it did him. If the dragon saw him now, he'd be blasted from its place atop the castle.

The crow perched in the window, but looked back several times as he spoke. "Right. When I say, you run straight for the doors and cut left through the palace. There's a hallway on that side that leads to a stairwell that should take you up through the ruins. Understand?"

Bastian nodded.

"Good. Do not stop. Not for anything. Stay still, she's looking this way."

For the first time, the way Aldram referred to the dragon caught his notice. *She.* He'd always spoken of the dragon as a girl. Bastian glanced up, but he saw nothing through the narrow slit of a window. It probably didn't matter; he didn't know how one might tell dragons apart, anyhow.

"Get ready," the crow whispered.

Bastian tensed, every muscle winding in preparation for the sprint to come. Long seconds slid by, thick with anticipation. His hands tightened on the hilt of his sword until his knuckles ached.

"Go!"

He bolted from the guard house and ran for the doors. His boots clacked against the cobbles and he winced with every few steps. Maybe it was better he didn't have armor. He was loud enough as it was.

"Go, go, go!" Aldram snarled as he darted past and vanished into the shadow of the castle's entry hall.

As if he wasn't going. Bastian ran with all his might, flying across the empty courtyard, his heart striking his ribs so hard he feared it might punch through.

The steps to the doorway, still littered with fragments of the shattered doors, loomed just ahead.

It wasn't far.

He fixed his eyes on the gap.

He could make it.

One by one, the hairs on the back of his neck began to prickle and his senses shrieked in warning. He skidded to a halt and flung his longsword toward the doorway, just as the ear-splitting crackle of lightning tore down from the clear blue sky.

It lanced past him and struck the sword as a shout tore free of Bastian's throat.

Sweat burst across his brow as the heat poured over him. His heart thundered off-rhythm and his ears rang, the reverberation only made worse by the long, angry scream that rose overhead, less monstrous and more human than he'd ever imagined, made more terrifying by both.

The dragon had seen him.

A cold lance of fear shot through him as his eyes darted upward and the massive black beast launched itself from the castle's peak.

He was almost there.

He had to run.

He darted forward and tried to snatch the longsword from the ground, but the blistering heat that radiated from the hilt stayed his fingers and he leaped past it instead.

The moment he dove in through the doorway, the dragon hit the ground. Bastian almost bit his tongue as the floor shuddered beneath his feet and knocked him to his knees.

"Get up!" Aldram roared beside his ear, clawing at his shoulder and beating his wings hard, as if that might pull him back to his feet.

Bastian scrambled up and bolted for the shelter of a hallway ahead. "Magic?" he cried. "You never said the dragon would have magic!" All he'd expected was fire, and this changed everything.

The crow flew right alongside him, hanging close. "What are you talking about? Of course she has magic! Isn't that the whole point? Killing her to break the curse—"

"And to rid the witch of power over Ceresia!" Bastian finished for him.

"Yes! Which is why—oh, Divine's mercy," Aldram groaned. Without warning, he dove in front of Bastian's face and fanned his wings to stop. "Divine's mercy, boy! I thought you knew, I thought that was why we were here!"

Bastian stumbled to a stop with his face no more than an inch from the bird's claws. They'd halted in the middle of an intersection with hallways branching off in every direction, and he scanned them all as he gasped for breath. "Knew *what*?"

"Heldin," Aldram said. "She's the witch *and* the wyrm!"

Eighteen

The witch.

The witch.

Bastian stumbled back a step, staring without seeing the crow in front of him.

The witch had killed his brother.

Had used that death to threaten his home.

Had stolen the tiny shred of joy that was his plan to marry Adelinde and live—if not happily ever after, then just to *live*, to be together and whole in a way he'd always known no other woman could make him.

That Florina could not make him.

He staggered back another step as he struggled to find words and came up short.

Aldram darted closer. "Get yourself together, lad."

"You knew? This whole time?" Bastian almost choked on his own voice.

"And thought it was why you suggested it! Mercy's sakes alive, you really thought coming over here and fighting a dragon for no blasted reason would help? Turn around! We have to get upstairs." Aldram lunged against his shoulder to turn him in the direction he was meant to go.

Bastian couldn't even think clearly enough to question it, his mind still stuck on the secret he only wished he'd known sooner. The whole time, the witch had been the one who destroyed their closest ally and threatened his homeland. He almost tripped over his own feet as the crow pushed him into motion. "Why did you let me come here?"

"Because, idiot, I thought you *knew*. I thought you were making a clever suggestion, coming up here to have the fight in the ruins, knowing she'd destroy half Ceresia if she used her magic to change shape." Aldram led the way up a wide flight of stairs that was all but clear of debris.

"How in all of heaven's name should I have known that?" Bastian protested.

"How in heaven's name did you not? You're the one who spent days bottled up in her office. You mean to say you didn't learn anything about her power while you were there?"

"I was a worm! How was I supposed to—" He stopped halfway up the stairs and swallowed a curse. "The sword!"

"We'll find another one," Aldram snapped. "You're not going back there unless you want to be toasted alive!"

Bastian opened his mouth to ask why the witch stayed in the form of a dragon when she could have easily followed him inside. Before a single word escaped, something struck the side of the castle so hard that even its foundation shuddered.

He staggered sideways and caught himself against the wall, lest he tumble back down the stairs. "What happened to creating legendary swords and names for them?"

The bird cawed in frustration. "Legends are for heroes, not boys that get roasted by walking straight into a dragon's maw. Move, boy! King's quarters. There's bound to be something there."

The king's quarters. Bastian knew where that was. He sprang up the rest of the stairs and darted down the hall. There was another flight of stairs, then a branch in the hallway that led to where his godfather's bedchamber had been. He only stumbled a little when the dragon struck the palace again.

When *Heldin* struck the palace, he corrected himself in his head. He struggled to wrap his mind around it. All that time, the witch had been playing his father for a fool.

He cleared the top of the second stairway and his heart sank.

Instead of the hallway he'd expected, there was a gaping hole where it once had been.

Aldram hissed an oath and darted across the void to explore the other side. He returned a moment later. "She hasn't seen where we've gone. I think you can make it across."

"Across what?" Bastian whispered, fearful his voice might carry if he didn't. It would only take a moment for the witch to circle the castle and catch him there, exposed.

"There's a ledge left against the standing wall." The crow looped around him and glided down to the stones he meant, supports for where beams had once been built into the walls. Here and there, shattered remnants of timbers still protruded from the stone.

"It's too narrow," Bastian said. "We're three floors up."

"Oh, so you'll run off to fight a dragon, but the moment you have to shimmy across a ledge, your sense of adventure is gone?" As if to highlight its ease, Aldram strolled along the narrow stone, his head bobbing as he took each exaggerated step.

"Easy for you, you're a fraction of my size." Bastian followed, though. He considered his options before he pressed his back flat against the wall and began to shimmy across. Stepping over the timbers would be difficult, but not impossible. Cold fear misted his brow with sweat as he moved, the toes of his boots hanging over a drop that promised death.

Aldram waited until he got close, then inched along at the same pace. "That's it. Just like that, Bastian. Keep going."

The encouragement should have helped. Instead, it reminded

him of the last time he'd visited Athanor, the last time he'd seen his godfather and trained by his side. It was hard to look at the place, to see the broken remnants of good memories scattered through the ruins. He stared straight ahead as he moved, unwilling to lower his gaze and see the destruction below. The ballroom would be down there. The yard where he and his brother had played and fought while their father walked with his ally and friend.

The cost of what the witch had stolen from him kept climbing higher.

"Almost there," Aldram coaxed.

Bastian's foot reached solid flooring and he all but shoved himself away from the wall to sprint the rest of the way. It wasn't far, and before he ran out of breath, they reached the door.

The room on the other side was dirty, the glass panes busted out of the leaded windows and letting in the weather outside. Leaves and debris lay scattered on the floor, but little had changed. The furniture remained upright, if the curtains and canopy that hung from the bed had grown tattered.

"A sword," Bastian breathed as his eyes darted around the space. "Where would he have a sword?"

Aldram swooped in to land atop a chest at the foot of the bed. "Try here."

A lock decorated the front of the chest. Bastian grimaced at the sight, but joined the bird beside it anyway. "It needs a key."

"Key, key..." Aldram scanned the room before he fluttered to a desk against the far wall. Old, damaged books sat atop it, alongside tarnished silver cups full of writing implements and wax seals. He knocked over the cups, one after another, and flung their contents to the floor one piece at a time.

Bastian tested the chest's lid, but it had not been exposed to the elements long enough to rot. The wood held fast, so he shoved himself up from the floor and joined the bird at the desk.

"Open that drawer." The crow pecked the wood above it, and he obliged. The moment it was open, Aldram hopped into the drawer and flung papers out. They drifted to the floor like falling leaves. "Ha!"

"Did you find it?" Bastian moved to the side to try and see, but the bird's glossy body blocked the way.

Aldram turned with a small, shiny brass key in his beak and deposited it into the prince's palm.

Bastian hurried back to the chest. The lock's mechanism was still good and it snapped open with ease, revealing all the finery Athanor's king had shut away.

"Under the red one, right there," the crow said.

"I don't see anything." Bastian dug deeper through the piles of fabric, all the same.

"What? How can you not see it? It's shiny, right there!"

The glint caught Bastian's eye a moment later and he went after it with both hands. It was as long as the chest, a fine two-handed blade in an ornately decorative scabbard. He could have groaned. "It's ceremonial!"

"It's sharp, I'm sure of it. Take it out. Give it a try." Aldram hopped along the edge of the open chest, his wings half spread to aid his balance.

Bastian stood and withdrew the blade from its sheath. It was almost longer than what he could manage, but he supposed that made sense. In his memory, the man was a giant, towering over everyone. The sword he held now promised that was a lie, but it did not change that his godfather had been taller than he was. He brushed his thumb against its edge and gasped when it cut. "It is sharp! How did you know?"

"What kind of idiot would keep a dull blade locked away? Come on, now." The bird launched himself toward the doorway.

The scabbard was so long, it would have gotten in his way. Bastian left it on the floor and carried the sword on its own. "Wait."

Aldram landed in the hallway and looked back.

"Before we go, I need..." Bastian's voice caught. He made himself breathe. "I need to ask a favor of you."

The look the bird gave him was complaint enough on its own. "Haven't I done enough for you already?"

"Please. This is important." He rested the blade flat against his shoulder so he could hold it with one hand. The other dove into the pocket of his coat and removed the suede coin purse. "I want... I want you to take this."

Aldram gaped. "Adelinde?"

Bastian held it out, his hand flat. "Take it, and take her somewhere safe."

"But you've brought her this far, don't you want—"

"If whatever I do here helps her, it'll help no matter where she is. I'm about to try and kill a witch in the shape of a dragon, Aldram. If this goes badly for me, I don't want her to be hurt." He tilted the purse so the strings fell toward the crow.

Aldram stared at it for a long time before he turned around.

Bastian thought he was going to object, but he loosened his wings instead.

"Tie it onto me," the crow instructed. "Like a little pack on my back. I'll carry her, but it means I can't help you against the witch."

"I don't expect you to. Just keep Adelinde safe. That's all I ask." Bastian cut the strings so he could tie them around Aldram's wings. Once it was fastened, it looked for all the world as if he wore a satchel on his back. He chanced a smile, then lifted his head. "Do you hear that?"

"I don't hear anything," Aldram said.

"Exactly. Where is the—"

Before Bastian could finish, the wall of the hallway exploded inward. He threw himself over the crow to shelter him—and Adelinde—as stones and debris rained down on them.

A massive black forepaw reached in and he turned the sword to ram its tip between the dragon's grasping fingers. The blade bit deep and the dragon jerked back with a furious shriek.

"Go!" Bastian shouted as the sword came free and dark

droplets spattered the stone. The moment they landed, plumes of smoke curled upward from the marks with a hiss.

Not blood.

Acid.

As if this wasn't hard enough already.

Aldram didn't wait for a second command. He launched himself, not toward the dragon, but back into the old king's quarters, where he dove out the broken window without a sound.

Good, Bastian thought. He shoved himself to his feet and ran to the edge of the hall, where the jagged edges of the hole in the wall framed him like shards of broken glass. He gripped the hilt of his godfather's sword in both hands. "Heldin!" he roared.

The black dragon's great horned head rose and her maw parted in a snarl, revealing more teeth than he could ever count. She surged toward the castle and slammed into the wall.

Wreckage fell all around him as her claws burrowed into the stone.

She raced up the wall like a lizard might scale a garden fence, and he barely leaped back in time to avoid her grasping claws.

He stabbed at the tendons in the back of her forepaw, but the scales were too hard, and the sword glanced off without leaving so much as a mark.

Bastian hissed. He had to get beneath her, to where he could reach her weak points, but the stairs were on the other side of the gap.

Maybe the answer *was* the gap. He gripped the sword and ran.

A rumble against the stones promised the dragon followed. Above it rose a harsh, monstrous cackle.

"You think you can best me, little prince?" The words throbbed in the air, a duotone of Heldin's honeyed speech and the dragon's booming voice.

The gap was just ahead. He shouted back as he ran. "You

took everything from me! My family, my freedom, the girl I loved!"

"And you speak as if you have nothing left to lose," she cackled. "Do you value your life so little?"

"I have no life left!" He looked to the wall, half expecting her to break through again.

Instead, she swung around the edge into the gap he was headed for, and her jaws dropped open wide.

Bastian threw himself against the floor as flames poured past her teeth and flooded the hall. They tore down his back, searing his skin through his clothes, and he'd never been so grateful to wear wool.

The moment the fire ceased, he sprang from the floor. A roar of fury tore from his throat as he brought the sword back and surged forward.

The dragon withdrew to avoid being struck.

It was exactly what he'd hoped for, and instead of swinging the blade at her, he skidded to a stop at the edge of the gap and flung the sword into what remained of the room on the level below. The moment his hands were free, he gripped the edge of the floor and swung down to launch himself to the castle's second story.

Heldin screeched in annoyance as he ran into the hallway again, beyond where she could reach. She seized the wall in both clawed forepaws and tore it wide open, then hunched down to wriggle inside. "You could have had everything!" she bellowed as her head snaked in after him. "You could have been king! All you had to do was follow my orders, to do as I say."

"Maybe you should learn to ask nicely," Bastian spat back.

"A sorceress asks for nothing. She takes what is hers!" the dragon screamed back, and a torrent of fire followed.

He dropped.

Flames swallowed the remaining carpeting and tapestries. They crackled and dropped ash as Heldin stared into the hall. Smoke cleared and her eyes slid to a hole in the floor.

"Then take this," Bastian said as he emerged beneath her.

He drove his sword into the soft flesh where her leg met her body.

The dragon roared with such intensity, stones toppled from the castle ruins to pelt her back and wings. Her head slammed into the ceiling as she tried to retreat and one curved horn snagged on a charred timber.

Bastian shoved harder and her roar climbed into an all-too-human shriek. Acid poured from the wound, cascading down his arms and half his chest, and his scream rose to join hers.

She thrashed, claws tearing at the stones around her as she tried to free her head, but he did not relent. Wild magic crackled across her skin and twisted around his hands, but Bastian did not let go.

He pressed on, farther and farther, until the sword's hilt struck her belly and the crumbling castle struck her wings.

Pain seared across half his body and as the last remnants of Athanor came down, he couldn't help but laugh.

He'd done it.

He'd won.

Stones pinned the dragon to the ground and the blade tore free of his grasp.

He shut his eyes and thought of Adelinde as the dragon collapsed above him, blotting out all light.

Nineteen

Pain woke him several times. Each time it roused him, muddy, blurred colors greeted his eyes and voices floated around his head. Bastian tried to focus, but it was like trying to grasp flower petals on the surface of water. The moment he reached for them, they swirled away.

Each time, someone brought him something to drink. It was bitter, laced with something that made him drift back to the dark and dreamless sleep that occupied his mind. He didn't want it, but he lacked the strength to fight.

Eventually, a ruddy glow replaced the darkness and he found his thoughts were clearer. The pain was not so severe, though he found he was more aware of its extent. The right side of his jaw, his neck, and all down his right side both ached and burned. His hands and arms, too, though the pain of the left was less severe. He opened his mouth to stretch his jaw. His skin pulled painfully and he stopped with a wince.

"Don't do that," Aldram chided. "She's only just finished changing your bandages. Won't do for you to sully them again as soon as they're on."

Bastian cracked open one eyelid. The crow sat on a gilded

perch in a familiar room, staring at him with a thoughtful intensity.

"Is he awake?" a soft, sweet voice asked. The familiarity of it made his heart leap.

"Adelinde!" He tried to sit up and regretted it immediately.

She almost dropped her mortar in her rush to put it down. It clacked against the table and she hurried to his bedside, both hands out to stop him.

He ignored the pain and grabbed her hands in his. Or, he tried; they were tightly wrapped and smothered with something slimy beneath the bandaging, and he could not properly grasp her with his hands resembling mittens.

Instead, she held him.

Everything hurt when he tried to move, but he couldn't bring himself to stay still. He dragged himself upright and pulled her into his arms. "You're alive," he rasped. His eyes stung and he blinked hard to clear them.

"And you nearly weren't," she said. She did not pull away, but settled on the edge of the bed and reached for his face. Her fingertips were soft and cool against his cheek and he savored the touch, though he dared not close his eyes.

"Neither was I," Aldram put in. "Darn near squished me when she came bursting out of that bag. Don't know what I was thinking, having you tie her onto me."

Adelinde laughed. "Oh, hush. You were fine."

"Better off than you, anyway." The bird glanced Bastian's way. "Found you smashed flat as a pancake under that dragon, and bathed in her blood, besides. I would have thought the witch would be forced to change back after you killed her."

"She bled acid." Bastian said it without thought, then looked down at himself. Ah. That was what the bandages were for.

"Your clothes kept the worst of it off you. If it hadn't, I... well, I don't know what I would have done." Fear and then sadness touched Adelinde's eyes. "But I'm afraid there's nothing else I can do to help you recover."

He brushed her face with his wrapped hands. "I don't care. You're all right, that's all that matters to me."

"Well, the good news is you should recover," Aldram said. "Though you may find the ladies aren't quite so interested in you as before."

"Aldram," Adelinde scolded.

"What? It's a benefit for you. No more having to chase down ingredients for magic potions to keep him from being married off." The crow almost cackled at the end. She batted at him as if to shut him up.

Bastian reached to claim her hand again. When he did, she cast him a guilty look.

"I did everything I could," she murmured. "All the best healing remedies I've learned, all the most comfortable salves. You've been recovering quickly, especially with the tea that puts you to sleep so your body can focus on healing, but..."

An odd tightness formed in his chest. "But?"

Tears turned her eyes glassy. They welled against her eyelashes until he found himself cursing the wrappings on his hands.

She looked away before the first tear fell. "I can't stop the scarring. The burns were too deep. It shouldn't cause you pain, though you may have some numbness in your hands and your face once it heals."

He tried to study her face, but she wouldn't look at him. His heart sank deeper than ever before, dragging him down into a canyon of silent fear. "I'm sorry," Bastian whispered. Pain unlike anything the dragon had wrought twisted his insides until he could scarcely choke out the words. "I... I understand. If you don't wish to look at me, then—"

Adelinde's eyes snapped back to his face. "What? No!"

"It's all right." It was anything but all right. "I understand. I promise. You're so beautiful, and I—"

She planted her fingers against his lips before he could finish and gave her head a firm shake. "Never. I would never leave you like that, Bastian. Not for any reason, least of all what Heldin's done to you."

He nudged her wrist to move her hand. "But—"

"By any shape or any name, I'll always love you," she said. "Just the same. Isn't that what you said?"

The tiniest flicker of hope sparked to life somewhere deep within him, and Bastian couldn't help but stare in wonder. "You heard me?"

The smile that curled her beautiful lips was almost timid. "I heard everything. All the way up until you tied me onto Aldram's back, that is."

The crow cleared his throat. "Right. And if the two of you are done, I'd like to move things along. The two of you are terribly uncomfortable to watch. Turns my stomach, really."

Adelinde laughed. "Nobody says you have to stay here, silly."

"Pah." Aldram spread his wings, but Bastian motioned for him to stay put.

"Wait. Please. I didn't have a chance to thank you. For working so hard to keep Adelinde safe, and for helping me, when I didn't know the way." He smiled, though it pulled uncomfortably along his jaw where Adelinde had coated him with salves and covered them with cloth. He'd have to see a mirror to determine what she'd done; his head wasn't wrapped, but the bandaging certainly stuck. "I appreciate everything, Aldram. But I admit I was hoping to see your curse was broken, too."

"Ah..." The crow batted a wing in dismissal. "That was never going to happen."

"But the witch was the one who laid it on you," Bastian said.

"Yes, but the terms of my curse were different. I thought it might unravel when I visited the... well, it hardly matters. I'm stuck this way, but at least I'm free. No more hiding, and I suppose no more hunting for answers, either. Curse-breaking doesn't work out for everyone, and some of us just have to deal with that." Aldram bowed his head, but he was sober for no more than a moment before he hopped closer. "Speaking of things to deal with, you're a hero now. There've been celebrations in the street since news of the dragon's death came. Wyrmsbane was on display in your father's receiving hall for a whole week before we convinced them to bring it back up here."

Bastian blinked twice. "Wyrmsbane?"

"Your sword, silly." Adelinde slid from the edge of the bed and crossed to the table. The blade lay there, and she bit her lower lip as she picked it up.

He motioned with his left hand for her to stop. Moving it hurt less. "Wait, you don't have to pick it up."

"I'm fine. I have my rings, see?" She grinned at him as she carried the sword to his bed.

And it was his bed, he realized. He'd been so distracted that he hadn't even noticed he lay in his own bedchamber, with Adelinde there to dote on him. A scarlet flush colored his cheeks.

"Now, don't be embarrassed," Aldram said. "You've earned it, boy. Both the sword and the title of hero that goes with it."

Adelinde started to put the sword on his lap, then thought better of it and laid it alongside him.

"It's a good sword." Bastian wished he could pick it up, but even were it not for the bandages, he did not yet know how well his hands would cooperate. It was still too long a blade for him, but he was grateful to have it. He didn't know how, but the dragon's blood had not damaged the blade at all. He craned his neck to marvel at its condition and his eyes latched to an emblem on the pommel. "Wyrmstooth? But this was King Dalmar's blade. Why does it have a symbol of Ceresia on its hilt?"

"Because it was a gift," his father's voice boomed from the doorway.

All of them looked up as the king's entourage slid into the room.

When Bastian saw who accompanied them, he thought he might be ill.

Florina.

Bernhard continued as if the presence of the witch's daughter were perfectly ordinary. "You know how dear a friend he was to me. To all of us. When our alliance was formally established, I gave him that blade as a gift. He carried it almost every day. If the dragon had not destroyed his body, I suspect we would have buried him with it."

The lily emblem drew Bastian's eyes again. It was fitting; a symbol of that which the sorceress had coveted was what destroyed her, in the end. "I should take it back to Athanor when I leave. Return it to the palace. Maybe to the royal tombs." Queen Emilia had been laid to rest there, and he suspected adding a representation of her husband to her grave was the kindest thing to do.

"I don't think you're going anywhere soon, lad," Aldram said.

"I have business in Athanor. Harrald's crew will be waiting." Truthfully, Bastian doubted they would wait at all. But he also doubted there was anything for them to divide. He'd made that offer under the assumption that the dragon was merely a monster, not knowing it was the witch in disguise.

Adelinde nodded, though. "We promised to meet them there. Aldram and I said we would take care of it after they helped us bring you back here."

"And there is business here for you to resolve," Bernhard added. His brows took a stern set and Florina stepped forward by his side.

Anger had never been a prevalent part of Bastian's life, but it surged in him now, swelling until he thought he might burst. He almost rose from the bed, but Adelinde put a hand against his uninjured shoulder and held him down. He exhaled hard through his nose and for a moment, he thought he might learn to breathe fire, too. "After everything I've been through, after everything I've done, how dare you bring her before me?"

"Peace," his father said, motioning with both hands for him to settle.

"Forgive me," Florina said at the same time. "I do not expect you to uphold the agreement our parents made."

"Good, because I won't," Bastian snapped.

She went on, unfazed. "I am glad to see you are in one piece, though I wish I could see you were well. I believe this will be the last time I see you at all. I've come to ask pardon for my mother's mistakes, nothing more."

He didn't want to grant her pardon. It was his father's job, not his. He glanced to Bernhard's frowning face as if to ask why she was there, instead of being dealt with before the throne.

Adelinde slid a hand up his shoulder, gently soothing. "Your mother's choices and actions are her own. Surely the king does not name you responsible for what has transpired, and it's not as if we've forgotten your help."

A thread of surprise sprang through Bastian's anger and gave him pause. He almost had forgotten. Had she helped Adelinde, too, or did she speak of the witch's daughter allowing them to escape? She'd said she heard everything. She would have heard that exchange in the kitchen, too.

Bernhard gave a slow nod. "She cannot be punished for her mother's wrongs. But the complacency and cooperation with those schemes are the girl's own doing, and after all that has happened, it seems most fair to let you decide what is adequate punishment."

Bastian didn't want to decide. He didn't want anything to do with her. Anger still simmered hot in his veins and he shut his eyes and breathed deep while he waited for it to settle.

Perhaps that was the best punishment—that he didn't wish to deal with her, that he never wanted to see her again. Ceresia would be his to rule and as long as she was part of his people, he was not sure he could be fair.

"The sorceress's estate," he said.

The king's brows rose.

"The crown will purchase it for half its value," Bastian continued. "All the witch's books, herbs, and tools will remain in the manor and will be destroyed or stored away at the crown's discretion, lest it fall into untrustworthy hands again. With the money from the estate's purchase, Florina will be able to start over anywhere and have a good life. She will leave Ceresia and be unwelcome to return."

The girl's face grew cool, but she nodded in acceptance.

"Very well." Bernhard rested a hand on her shoulder and beckoned the guards who had escorted them. "Such a task will take several weeks to sort, but it will be arranged. Take her back to the estate now, allow her to collect only her things."

The guards bowed and made space for Florina to join them. The room remained quiet until she was gone.

The moment the door closed behind her, Aldram harrumphed. "Well, she's not welcome in Athanor either, that's for certain."

"I don't think anyone will wish to settle in Athanor for a long time," Bernhard said. "Not while the dragon's body remains."

"Ill omens," the crow agreed. "We'll resolve business, but rebuilding the north... that problem will take some time."

The king nodded and rested his hands against his hips. "Which I suppose leaves you to deal with." He sighed as he studied Adelinde, who lowered her head and blushed. "You'd already saved my son once, when that fever came upon him during the forest hunts. Now, you've saved him twice more. From the witch, and from the wyrm. What reward do you seek?"

Bastian reached for her hand and gripped it the best he could, his wrapped fingers folded tight around hers. He already knew what she wanted. He'd tried to give it before, but that had started all this. After all they'd been through, he wasn't sure she would forgive him for his folly.

"If it would please you, Your Majesty," Adelinde said slowly, her head still down. She dared not look the king in the eye. "I would ask that you allow Bastian to keep a promise he made to me, many years ago."

Bernhard's mustaches twitched. "Which is?"

"We wish to be married," Bastian finished for her. "With your blessing."

His father stared at them so long, he half expected a denial. At last, the king blew out a long sigh and gave a helpless shrug. "You defied me, but in doing so, you saved my country, avenged your brother, and served justice to the beast who laid waste to my greatest ally and killed my dearest friend. Who am I to refuse what your heart desires?"

Bastian's mouth fell open before he could stop it. "You mean it? You give your blessing?"

"I do," his father said. "May the two of you lead a long and happy life."

Adelinde laughed, the sound rich with both joy and relief, and her dark eyes sparkled when she turned his way.

More than anything, Bastian wished he could pick her up and spin her, cradle her in his arms and celebrate the moment as it truly deserved. But his bandaged body protested when he tried to move, so he settled for what he could do.

He cradled her face in both his wrapped hands and kissed her, soft and sweet.

Twenty

It was several weeks before Adelinde decided Bastian had recovered enough to travel. The medicines she made improved his healing to the point the palace's own medics had begun to come to her with questions. She appreciated the respect, yet the attention left her flustered, and Bastian and Aldram had taken it upon themselves to chase them away when they decided she'd had enough.

The three of them rode together in an ornately gilded carriage—or, she and Bastian did. Aldram chose to ride on the roof, alongside their supplies. Empty wagons snaked along behind them, all of them ready to carry back whatever they could recover from Athanor's ruins.

The decision to remove wealth from the ruined country had struck her as odd, but it was a choice made in a meeting she had not been privy to, and everyone assured her it was for the best. Most of Athanor's people had traveled south and taken shelter in Ceresia when their home fell. Whatever treasure their expedition retrieved now was to be dispensed to those refugees, Bastian had explained, enabling them to return home and rebuild if they desired.

What would become of Athanor itself, no one seemed to have decided. The capital could not be reclaimed; the acid from the dragon's remains had seeped into the soil, rendering it inhospitable for years to come. Adelinde suspected the territory would be put beneath Bastian's control and eventually be swallowed by the expansion of Ceresia's borders.

"You're looking very serious," Bastian remarked playfully.

Adelinde blinked at the window before she turned toward him. He hadn't stopped smiling since the day he'd awakened and his father had granted permission for them to wed, and as he healed, that smile only brightened. Many of his bandages had been retired, though enough remained that it had been deemed best that she accompany him on this expedition and act as his personal healer, ensuring nothing he did might aggravate his recovery.

Most of it had gone well. The scarring on his face was not as bad as she'd feared it might be, and though the skin was more taut than she would have liked, it did not seem to bother him.

"Sorry." She chanced a smile of her own when she realized he was still waiting for a response. "I was just wondering what we're supposed to do if we can't find enough to make it worth everyone's time."

"You mean for Harrald and the others? If it goes poorly, I've already drafted letters for each of them, inviting them to visit the palace and receive payment for their services directly from my father's treasury. It won't be as much as a third of a dragon's treasure, but it would be generous, more than enough to make it worth their time." He shrugged, unbothered.

Seeing him calm and relaxed was a relief. He'd always been so cheerful; in the wake of their curses and the witch's death, she had noticed an unfamiliar anger inside him that she did not know how to address. It had abated somewhat after Florina's departure, but parts of it lingered.

For as many scars as he had on the outside, she supposed

there were some on the inside, too. It struck her as unfair. She had worked so hard to spare him, yet he had suffered in the end. She rubbed her hands and her gold splint rings clinked.

The sound drew Bastian's attention and he nodded toward them. "That reminds me. I overheard you telling Aldram your knee still hurts. You were injured during your quests?"

Adelinde's hand went to her knee out of reflex, but she smiled. "Not severely. It aches, but I've had worse. It's not the first time something has bent the wrong way and I don't think it will be the last."

"I'll have a brace made for you as soon as we get home," he promised.

"I'll be all right."

"I know you will, because I'll have a real brace made and you'll rest so it can heal properly. Look, I think we've made it." He leaned closer to the window to peer outside. The way he seamlessly flowed from one subject to another was so classically Bastian that she could not help but grin.

The carriage creaked to a halt and a moment later, the footman had the door open. They'd parked facing the ruins of Athanor's palace, and a group of men both familiar and strange moved to greet them.

Bastian slid from the carriage first, then turned to offer his arms. Adelinde refrained from leaping into them, reminding herself that some of his injuries remained. Instead, she merely laid her hands in his and let him help her down.

"Begging your pardon, your lordship," Harrald said as they climbed out. "It seems I may have, ah... underestimated your nobility." His eyes skimmed the carriage, lacquered with the royal crest, and his nerves showed through. He was still a highwayman, after all, and Bastian would have been well within his right to have Harrald and all his men arrested.

"An easy mistake, given the state I was in when we met. I see you received my letter." Bastian had been uncertain how to contact the brigands to arrange for treasure to be divided; it had been Aldram who offered a solution. The crow had carried the message and delivered it himself, after he found the men in the woods.

"It's good to see you again," Adelinde put in. She owed the men a debt of her own after they'd braved the acid and the ruins to help her rescue Bastian after the witch was slain. With luck, whatever came of today would be a rich enough reward.

The brigand gave her a polite nod. "Aye. You, too, my lady. Congratulations on your betrothal. I was pleased when the bird told me you got your happy ending. Let's get down to business, though, shall we? I've got news I think your lordship—ah, Your Highness—will enjoy."

"You are welcome to call me Bastian, friend. And I assumed you had news, considering how your numbers have grown." Bastian nodded toward the men who stood about the ruins behind Harrald's back. Rather than the five men who had assisted them before, they had to number at least fifty.

"Don't you worry about them," Harrald laughed. "Let me climb up with your driver, there, and take you to what we've found. You're going to love this."

Adelinde raised a brow, but did not argue when Bastian waved for her to get into the carriage again. "What do you suppose he's talking about?" she asked in a murmur. She hardly had any notion, herself. Even with all the men the brigands had added to their ranks, they could not have hoped to harm the crown prince when he traveled alongside several hundred soldiers.

"Not a clue. Here, scoot over. Let me sit next to you." He shoved her silk skirts out of the way, settled close by her side, and draped an arm around her shoulders.

A soft blush warmed her cheeks, but she leaned into him, all the same. Her ear pressed to his chest and she marveled at the sound of his heartbeat, so strong and steady. It was comforting, right in a way nothing had ever been, and she was content to stay there until the carriage finally halted again.

When they climbed out this time, they were at the foot of one of the cliffs a decent way north of what had been Athanor's capital.

"Here?" Bastian asked, confused.

A gruff laugh answered and Harrald leaped down from the front. "Just wait, Your Highness. You'll see."

Their procession halted and both soldiers and men from Harrald's crew leaped from the wagons. The brigands led the way to the rocky wall, where they seized a stone. Against all odds, it moved when they pushed it, and Adelinde gasped when they revealed a passage.

"Lanterns," Harrald called. A dozen men produced and lit them and led the way into the dark.

Bastian laced his rough fingers with Adelinde's and started forward with no hesitation. He only slowed when soldiers swarmed forward to escort them.

A shadow swooped by and made Adelinde's heart leap before she realized it was Aldram. He circled around to land on her shoulder, mindful of his claws. "I'd forgotten this was here," he admitted, sheepishly.

She lifted a hand to scratch beneath his beak, pleased when he stretched into her touch. "What is this place?"

Aldram hummed softly. "An old mine shaft. Closed down a good twenty years ago or so, after the foreman of the operation determined the mine was thoroughly exhausted."

"What were they digging for?" Bastian's voice echoed off the walls and grew louder. He flinched at the sound.

"Iron, mostly," the crow said. "It was never a good quality ore, but we mixed it with carbon to make—good heavens, what is *that*?"

"Here it is, Your Highness," Harrald announced as he stepped into a broad opening and swept an arm wide. "A third for me, a third for you, and a third for that bird of yours."

A low murmur of awe swept through the soldiers ahead of them before Adelinde reached the end of the corridor and saw what the men had found. She raised a hand to her mouth, but not even a breath escaped.

Instead of an ordinary cavern, the mine shaft opened into a great crater filled with gold and jewels so wide that the sight made her knees weak.

"Steady," Bastian whispered. He snaked an arm around her waist and held her firmly to his side.

Adelinde held on to him, too. Forget what she'd ever seen; it was more wealth than she'd ever imagined. More men with lanterns filtered in behind them. Some were already on their way down into the pit where the treasure waited, though none were in a hurry.

"There's no way all this is from Athanor," Aldram murmured. "Even the royal vaults were only a fraction of this size."

"Don't know where it all came from, but it's ours now," Harrald almost cackled.

"I can't believe you waited," Adelinde said. In the weeks it had taken Bastian to recover, the brigands could have made themselves rich.

Then again, perhaps they had. If they'd spent every day loading their pockets, they still could not have made a dent in what lay before them. She stepped away from Bastian's side and looked for a safe way down.

The brigand led the way. "There are coins here from twenty different countries, at least. There's no way to know how long your witch was playing her intimidation game, but it looks like Athanor and Ceresia weren't her first targets."

"Then why store it here?" Aldram asked.

Bastian shrugged. "Centrality? That was why she was most interested in us. We're both landlocked, which can be a benefit in its own way. Especially with powers like hers. It's hard to move large forces across great expanses of land, and all her enemies would be right on the surface, where a dragon could easily wipe them out."

Adelinde knelt at the edge of the hoard and slid a hand over the treasure. It was more than just gold; bronze statues jutted from the heap at haphazard angles and gemstones glittered everywhere. "Do we know how old she was? She looked young enough, but what if she wasn't? She could have spent lifetimes amassing this sort of wealth."

"Yet at the end of the day, it got her no closer to holding the power she desired," Aldram said.

She plucked a gold chain with a fat ruby on its end from the pile and draped it over the bird's head. "Look. So much for protecting against evil, hmm?"

The crow scoffed, but puffed up his chest. "You can't prove it didn't help a little. We're all here now, aren't we?"

"And the evil is gone, at least for the moment." Bastian grinned. "Harrald, divide your men into groups. I'll match each one with mine. We'll go section by section and work to divide everything fairly. Whatever treasure is recognizable as being from Athanor should be returned to Athanor's people, so sort it into my share."

"And mine," Aldram put in.

Adelinde frowned at him.

"What? I'm Athanorian, too." He looked away, feigning innocence.

"You're spoiled, is what you are. I can't believe you're getting a whole cut of this to yourself." She draped another chain around his neck, then stood and dusted her hands together.

"Choose something," Bastian said. "Pick a treasure to keep for yourself."

She raised her brows. "I already did."

He tilted his head, like a puppy that didn't understand, until she pointed at his chest. He laid a hand against his heart and laughed. "That was already yours, Nightingale. Pick something else."

Adelinde giggled. "Fine. But only because you insist." She contemplated the pile of treasure for a moment before she dared to lift a foot. It felt wrong to tread upon something so valuable, but it stretched on in mounds beyond what she could comprehend. Somewhere, there had to be something she might want to keep.

Jewelry of every sort lay mixed with coins and chunks of melted gold. Silver tea sets peeked out from underneath circlets, and someone had draped chains of gold and strings of pearls around the necks of statues. It was odd; Heldin had always struck her as powerful, but human. There was nothing human about the hoard of treasure she walked across now. Perhaps taking the form of a creature meant taking on some of its attributes, too.

Yet she felt nothing like a worm. She never had. Even when she'd been curled up inside Bastian's coin purse, she had felt like herself—trapped inside a strange and different body, but still her own self, still devoted to loving him and fearful that her existence and his love for her might bring him harm.

In a way, it had. She had tried apologizing for the harm that had befallen him, but he wouldn't hear it. It had been his choice, he'd said; something he would have done to earn her hand regardless of the curse.

Adelinde halted mid-stride and turned toward a sculpture of some forgotten warrior. A painting leaned against its knees. Odd. She'd seen no other paintings, and as far as she had known, dragons did not favor flammable treasure.

"That goes back to Athanor," Bastian said.

She hadn't realized he followed her. She flashed a nervous smile over her shoulder, then waved a hand toward the canvas. A portrait of royals, she assumed, though neither the man nor the woman in the image wore crowns. "They look familiar."

"You probably saw them in the palace. That's Emilia, the late

Queen of Athanor. And that's Dalmar, King of Athanor and my godfather."

Adelinde cocked her head to the side and fidgeted with the gold rings on her fingers. "She's not your godmother?"

"They were married after I was born, after Athanor and Ceresia were already allies." Bastian tucked his hands into his pockets and nodded toward the painting. "But she died young. Just before the fall of Athanor, if I remember right. I wonder, sometimes, if things would be different if Dalmar hadn't been grief-stricken when the dragon appeared. I think he loved her almost as much as I love you. They were always painted holding hands like that, see?"

She looked when he pointed, despite the odd, prickling sensation that crawled up her neck. "Hands," she murmured. They were painted in frame, their fingers interlaced, his strong.

Her heart dropped.

"Aldram," she gasped. She spun on her heel and scrambled back the way she'd come.

"Wait!" Bastian shouted. "What are you—"

"Aldram!" She skidded down the side of a pile of coins and winced when she fell. Her backside hit the metal hard, jostling her bones and promising to bruise.

The crow sat at the peak of another pile, examining his reflection in a silver cup as he tried to position a circlet far larger than he was atop his head.

Adelinde leaped forward and seized him in both hands.

An ungainly squawk tore out of his beak and he kicked hard. "Hey, hey! Unhand me! It's mine by right! One third of the spoils!"

"Shut up," she snapped, and her tone was so sharp that he went still.

Her feet slipped in the gold as she tried to scale the heap again without the help of her hands. She squeaked, but then Bastian was there, catching her by the arms and helping her up the hill. Confusion twisted his features, but he didn't argue as she regained her footing and tore away from his grasp with the crow held before her.

They slid to a stop and she fell to her knees before she planted the bird atop the treasure.

"What are you—?" he protested, but she put a hand on his feathered back and spun him to face the portrait. He froze.

"Adelinde," Bastian gasped as he came after her. He stopped, his scarred hands out as if to catch her or stop something, but his feet locked into place.

Aldram sat transfixed before the painting. Threads of golden light drifted across the surface of his sleek feathers and slowly, his beak parted. "The flame, and... true love's face..."

"That's why you knew the way into the castle," Adelinde said. "Why you knew everything about Athanor, why you wanted into the royal tomb. Because that's you, isn't it? King Dalmar?"

Magic cracked through the room like thunder, drawing shouts from the men who worked to divide the treasure. Light shot across the crow's feathers and wind burst outward, forcing Adelinde to stumble back. Bastian caught her as the light of power that swallowed Aldram's form grew too bright to look at and they both turned away, shielding their eyes.

A second boom shook the cavern and coins spilled from their piles, jingling in a cheerful chorus that went on for what felt like ages.

When the melody finally grew still, everything was silent.

Adelinde peeled her hands away from her eyes.

Where Aldram had been, a man with his dark hair and beard shot with white knelt before the portrait, tears streaking down his face.

All around them, soldiers and brigands stood staring.

Slowly, he lifted a hand and trailed a finger across the queen's image. "My name," he whispered. "I remember my name."

Bastian bolted forward and almost leaped upon him in a hug.

The king received it with a roar of delight and opened an arm to Adelinde, too.

More sedately than her sweetheart, she slipped near enough to accept the embrace.

"Adelinde," Dalmar laughed. "You've done it. I didn't think —I didn't believe—by the Divine, I didn't even tell you!"

"You're alive," Bastian cried. "All these years, you—" He stopped short and his face grew stormy. "You called me an idiot!"

"Well you didn't exactly prove me wrong," the king replied. "You didn't even recognize my voice. It was Adelinde who did it, who figured it all out. I can't believe it, girly. You truly are a curse breaker, aren't you?"

She giggled, though her eyes stung with a joy she could not explain. "But what was it? What did I do? You never told me the terms of your curse!"

"*True love's face and true love's flame,*" Dalmar recited, "*will shatter the curse when you remember your name.*"

"That's not fair," Bastian said. "I told you all about yourself when we were in the woods and nothing happened."

The king shook his head. "I couldn't remember then. I couldn't remember because I wasn't here, looking at her. It's all tied together, and... oh, Divine have mercy, Emilia. How could I let all this happen?" He heaved such a sigh that his shoulders slumped.

Adelinde gently touched his face, smoothing his beard the way she'd smoothed his feathers. "You can't blame yourself for what the witch has done."

"Oh, I can. And I will, for some time. But this... this is better than I ever hoped for. Thank you, Adelinde. Both of you. Thank you, from the bottom of my heart. I don't think I can ever repay you." Dalmar squeezed them both tight, then finally let go.

Bastian sat back on the mountain of gold and pulled Adelinde down with him. "I'm sure there's some way."

"I can think of one," she said as she nestled into Bastian's arms and let herself be held. There was nothing else like it, no greater comfort she had ever known, and her heart swelled with a joy that would never be matched. "Come back to Ceresia and be a part of our wedding."

Dalmar laughed. "Adelinde, dove, there is nothing I would love more."

Epilogue

The path outside Adelinde's window had grown over with weeds. She watched them bob in the wind as her assistants carried the last crates of her belongings from the cottage she'd inhabited for longer than she could remember.

Part of her wished to pull the weeds and leave the space bare, ready for Bastian's feet, the way it had always been. Yet there was no longer any need. They covered the hard-packed earth like a scab, unsightly, but a sign of mending. In its own way, that made them beautiful, too.

The last of her plants had already been marked with colored string. The royal gardeners would be along to retrieve them soon, or else tend them until autumn, when they could be transplanted without fear of damage. Bastian had set aside a space in the palace gardens for her herbs and flowers, and there was an adjacent room reserved for her use, where she could hang things to dry or mix her tinctures in peace. It was a thoughtful gift, but then, that was Bastian.

"My lady," a guard prompted.

She expected to be told it was time to leave. Instead, she lifted her head and the man pointed to a cluster of people on the road. A handful of soldiers wrapped around a young woman

Adelinde had never thought she'd see again, much less outside her own home.

As if she shared the sentiment, Florina greeted her with a nervous smile. "Today's the day. The sale of my mother's estate has been finalized, so I am going south."

The coast, Adelinde concluded. Whether that meant Florina would settle there or seek a new home even farther away, she did not know, nor did she care. She searched for words, but before she found any, the witch's daughter raised the wooden box she carried in her arms.

"I brought you a gift," Florina said. "A wedding gift, I suppose, since that's tomorrow. It seemed that you ought to have it, after everything you've been through."

Adelinde tried not to frown. Rather than accepting the gift herself, she motioned for one of the guards to take it. The armored man took the box from Florina's arms and slid open its top. Inside, the wyrmstooth lily rested, its head heavy with new buds.

"You are the one who retrieved it, after all," Florina added with a sheepish smile. "It won't be useful unless you mean to make poison, but you never know. It may serve some purpose. It's particularly toxic to dragons, though I hope you never have to deal with one of those again."

"Thank you." Adelinde had never imagined adding such a thing to her garden, but she supposed it fit. A symbol of Ceresia, of what it once had been, of what it might become under Bastian's rule. She could still hardly fathom that she would be given a crown of her own, never mind the title of queen consort that waited for the day Bastian took the throne. Marrying him was all she had ever desired, yet somehow, she had never considered what duties that would bring.

The witch's daughter smiled with genuine warmth. "I hope it aids you, somehow."

"I believe it will." Over time, the palace gardens could be filled with the lily, restoring a symbol that was all but lost.

Adeline tried to smile back, but found she could not. "I admit I never thought we would speak again, but I appreciate that you took the time. I never had the chance to properly thank you for your assistance in helping us escape. You had every opportunity to stop us, when Bastian fled with me in his hands, but you didn't."

Florina's cheerful mask faltered. "He loves you. No force could ever hope to stand in the way of that, no matter what my mother desired."

So few had spoken of Heldin or her schemes after the dragon was slain. The woman's death had become a thing of legends, whispered to children as a story of triumph, or shared raucously at tavern tables for travelers who had not yet heard. But it was the death that mattered; not her life or her purpose.

Somehow, Adelinde had never considered that Heldin's purpose and her daughter's had not been the same. "And what about what you desired?"

Florina shrugged. "I never gave it much thought. When I was young, I wanted to become a sorceress, like she was. But the power to change shape comes with a price, and I was not willing to pay it. After that, I suppose I never had much purpose."

Curiosity itched behind Adelinde's ears, but she motioned for the guard to place the lily's box among her things on the wagon before she asked. "What sort of price?"

"The longer someone stays in a borrowed form, the more they become that creature for real," Florina said. "I'm sure you noticed it. Over the years, my mother grew angry. And greedy, for both gold and power. Pleasing her grew exhausting and I never had time for anything else. There was always something new to fix, some mistake she'd made when her temper got the better of her. For all that she desired power, she didn't know how to wield it, whether big or small. She took Athanor, but she frightened off its people, and what good is a country without citizens? She negotiated a marriage between myself and Bastian to gain people beneath her power, but cursed him in a fit of rage, and what sort of husband is a worm?"

Adelinde stifled a laugh behind her hand. "Not a good one."

"Not at all," Florina agreed. A small sparkle of amusement lit her eyes, and for the first time, Adelinde considered that had things been different, perhaps the two of them would have gotten along. Both of them bore some sort of magical talent; both of them carried a burden of heritage that stood in their way.

But only one of them had conquered it.

A moment passed before Florina cleared her throat. "Just so you know, I never had any desire to take him away from you. You've earned every bit of what you have now."

"Thank you." That, at least, Adelinde could say with honesty. "I hope you find some new desire, wherever you end up."

"Thank you. And congratulations." The witch's daughter curtsied, then motioned for the guards to lead the way. It was only then that Adelinde saw the pack mule one of them led, the creature weighted down with the belongings Florina had been allowed to keep. They pressed on, headed south, and Adelinde wondered what Florina might have done with the lily if her cottage hadn't been along the way.

"Well, that was sweet enough to be sickening," a familiar voice drawled from the other side of the garden.

Adelinde turned. Aldram—or, King Dalmar, rather—lounged against her uneven garden fence, a retinue of borrowed bodyguards at his back. He wore less fine of clothing than what he deserved, but she thought they suited the version of him she knew. She knew little of what he was like as a king.

She planted her hands on her hips. "Well, maybe you could learn something by watching. It wouldn't hurt *you* to be sweet once in a while."

"Ah. Sweet's not my way, dove. You should know that by now." A sparkle lit his brown eyes, all the same, and he pointed at the garden. "You grow all this yourself?"

"With some help from my mother," she conceded.

"I surely would have liked to meet her. Maybe then I'd be able to figure out what you are." His shoulders hunched as he scrutinized her face.

Adelinde snorted. "What's that supposed to mean?" The friendly tone she took with him made the guards shift in discomfort, but she'd grown too used to the playful ribbing to give it up now that she knew who he was. It wasn't as if he seemed to mind, either; the way he kept on invited that sort of banter, and his eyes lit up every time she talked back. She was glad. He'd remained the same kind of annoying-yet-fun uncle figure he'd made himself while he was a bird, and she dreaded to think of how quiet things would be when he returned to the ruins of Athanor to rebuild.

Dalmar squinted. "Dryad, maybe? Some sort of woodland fae. Diluted, but there. I'd bet my kingdom on it."

She snorted in response. "Nobody would want to wager anything for your kingdom until you're done fixing it."

"Maybe a harpy," he concluded dryly.

"That's not even a fae creature."

"No, just unpleasant." Dalmar smirked, but went on. "Are you done down here? Bastian was getting antsy. He sent me to see what was keeping you, but given how many little tassels you've got tied on these plants and how many there still are, I suppose I ought to go tell him to give up waiting."

"I've just finished. I suppose I could walk back with you now." She gave her garden one last look. The palace was where she belonged now; she wished she could linger, but this was no longer her home. She had outgrown it in the same way the weeds grew over Bastian's spot outside her window.

Dalmar's expression softened. "It's hard, isn't it? Leaving the place you always thought was home?"

She slipped through the gate to join him. "Yes, but it's different for me. You get to go back to Athanor when all this is over." Her retinue stayed behind to finish loading the small wagon with all the pieces of her former life.

"True, but I'll be alone. Be grateful for what you're getting, girly. Dreams rarely come without costs." He straightened and offered his arm.

Adelinde could not argue with that. She accepted with a small smile. "Speaking of costs, you never did tell me how you came to be cursed."

"Didn't I?" Dalmar asked, surprised. "Well, it's not all that exciting. At first, the witch wanted money and land. I gave her both. Then she changed the terms. After that, she wanted to be queen of Athanor, but the only way for that to happen was for me to betray my people or my wife, and I wasn't going to do either. I'm a real believer in true love, you see, but also in responsibility. Had I known then she could turn into a dragon, I might have shirked some of the latter." He winked.

She laughed. "You are a bit of a scoundrel, aren't you?"

"So I've heard. Now," he sighed as he led her toward the road that meandered through the village, and his guards rearranged themselves to accommodate them both. "On the subject of untold stories, why don't you tell me how you met Bastian to begin with?"

Adelinde grinned, but ducked her head as a rosy blush colored her cheeks. "Well, I suppose it started when King Bernhard took Erich out on a hunt in the forest, but left Bastian behind, as he was feeling unwell..."

And so the wedding followed the next day, a ceremony as remarkably ordinary as Adelinde ever could have hoped. The same dressmaker Bastian hired to clothe her for the ball made her gown, a lavish piece of silk in a shade of blue to match the crown prince's eyes.

In the absence of her father, King Dalmar escorted Adelinde up the chapel's aisle, and the smiles she and Bastian shared as they recited their vows left no guests present without tears.

"You know," Bastian whispered as the priest bound their wrists with a silk cord, "I said I'd love you by any name, but I admit I'm glad I'll get to love you by one we share."

"And what about by shape?" she asked with a grin.

He chuckled as the knot was tied, binding them together for the years yet to come. "That will never change. But let's try to keep to this one, shall we?"

Adelinde giggled in agreement and leaned forward at the priest's cue.

Of all the tender stolen kisses she had shared with Bastian, none had ever been so sweet.

About the Author

Beth Alvarez has enjoyed writing since childhood and is a ravenous reader.

A visual arts major, Alvarez has worked as a freelance web designer, graphic designer, illustrator, and video game programmer. When not writing, she enjoys drawing, playing video games, driving, and sewing for her unusual collection of Asian ball-jointed dolls. Her collection can be seen on her YouTube channel, Lomi's Playground.

Raised in southern Illinois, she now resides in the suburbs of Memphis, Tennessee with her husband, daughter, and a very mean cat.

If you enjoyed this story, consider signing up for Beth's author newsletter so you'll never miss a future release:

https://www.ithilear.com/newsletter.html

Books by Beth Alvarez

ARTISAN MAGIC

The Assassin's Bride

The Spymaster's Prize

The Artificer's Wife

The Maiden's Merchant

SNAKESBLOOD SAGA

Serpent's Mark

Serpent's Tears

Serpent's Bane

Serpent's Wake

Serpent's Crown

Serpent's Blood

SPECTRUM LEGACY

Spectrum Blade

Paragon of Fire

Paragon of Water

Paragon of Light

Paragon of Shadow

Spectrum Legacy

WESTKINGS HEIST

To Steal the World

To Steal the Crown

To Steal the Queen

9 781952 145315